JUST LIKE JESSE JAMES

a novel

TIM McGREGOR

Perdido Pub
TORONTO

Copyright © 2017 Tim McGregor

ISBN-13: 978-0992040321

ISBN-10: 0992040329

"Tell Alan Pinkerton and his detectives to look for us in Hell."

– Jesse James, 1873

October, 1880

THE LID OF THE coffin was handed up out of the open grave and set aside on a bed of clover. The penny nails sticking out of the rough-milled pine looked like the crooked teeth of some oblong mouth.

The man kneeling at the edge of the excavated hole held the lantern in his hand and watched as the man down in the grave lashed a kerchief over his face. The gunnysack cloth did little to filter out the noxious gases rising from the occupant of the pine casket.

"Look away, Rufus," said the man in the grave. "No reason for you to look on this."

The other man removed his hat and shrugged. "The departed is nothing new to these eyes, Dingus."

"Suit yourself," said the man in the grave.

"I aim to."

With the kerchief in place, the man in the grave shrugged and bent to his work.

A square of sail canvas was unfolded and spread over the small corpse and then the kerchiefed man looked up at his companion above. Three bulging satchels were handed down and nestled at the foot of the casket. The cinch cord on one of the bags had loosened and coins of gold rattled onto the pine boards. The kerchiefed man returned them to the satchel and drew the cord tight again.

One last item was passed down, bundled in damp oilcloth. The man in the grave unfolded the greased material to inspect the pistol within; a long-barreled Schofield with the cylinder removed and the metal oiled for storage. Satisfied, he wrapped it up again and tucked it alongside the sacks. A box of dry cartridges was added to the trove before the man gathered up the ends of the sail canvas and draped it over the body. His eyes were watering from the death gases and he hoisted himself out of the grave to get away from the miasma. The other man lowered the coffin lid into the hole and climbed down himself, causing a small landslide of sandy grit to tumble into the casket. Holding his breath, he quickly fitted the lid onto the coffin and hammered in the penny nails and scrambled out of the hole. They had but one shovel between them and they took turns backfilling the dirt. Neither man spoke, communicating to his co-conspirator with only a grunt or a nod of the head. The only voices heard was that of the crows, cawing at them from the tree branches above.

Present Day

1

An open grave - High lonesome youth - Grandmother Traven - Green plastic turf and a pink carnation - The farm - Sundry chattels - Bickering siblings - What is owed, what is due

THE DOGWOOD PETALS of late May blew through the headstones of the prim cemetery, scattering across the unnatural green of the plastic turf skirted around the open grave. A large casket of burled mahogany lay poised on boards above a perfectly oblong hole in the earth where some of the petals tumbled into, vanishing from sight. There was a wreath on a stand composed of mostly plastic flowers, to which a few of the mourners shook their head in disdain or embarrassment. They couldn't spring for a full arrangement of fresh flowers, they would whisper later at the luncheon. How disrespectful can you get?

Upright among these solemn-faced mourners stood Lee Traven, situated between his stoically firm parents in the same dark suit that he had worn for graduation. It felt stifling in the May sun and the buttoned collar chafed his Adam's apple. He listened impatiently to the priest droning on over his grandmother's casket without hearing any of the vicar's words. He was too busy scanning his eyes over the assembled congregants at the burial. All family; a menagerie of aunts and uncles and cousins of varying ages. Some were openly weeping while others cleared their throats and stifled the urge to look at their phones.

He surveyed the mourners again, this motley assembly of relations, for one face in particular but hers was not to be seen. Did she not make it home for Grandma's funeral? Did she not care or was she too busy with school to hop on the bus and make the four-hour trip back to this shit stain of a town?

The priest had ceased his monotonous droning, closing the good book and lowering his head, but now lonely Aunt Pauline was singing. A mournful tune wrung out in her high-pitched voice, the words catching short as the emotion clenched her vocal chords. Lee frowned, pulling the collar from his sticky throat.

A sharp elbow jabbed into his ribs. His father, hissing under his breath without even looking at him.

"Quit fidgeting. Show some respect."

Loud enough for his mother to hear but she kept her eyes on Aunt Pauline, caught up in the funeral rapture. Still, Lee felt her stiffen at his side as if the warning was meant for her too. This was a pattern Lee had come to recognize intuitively in his eighteen years; his father's grumbling admonitions were meant for everyone within earshot regardless of who they were directed at.

Lee struggled to remain still as the hymn finally ended and the man in the dog collar concluded the service.

"As we consign the remains of Marion Rose Traven to the earth," the priest said, his voice failing against the wind whistling off the open plain beyond the cemetery, "we commend her spirit to the Almighty with a last prayer. The day is now passed. Jesus, keep me within thine sight, and save me from the coming night."

The priest closed his prayer book, beads of sweat dimpling on his upper lip. "Before we go," he said, "the family would like to remind everyone that the reception following the service will be held at the farmhouse. All are welcome."

The priest took a step back on the fake green turf and the attendant from the funeral home flipped a switch on the electrical winch behind him. The coffin began to lower into the grave. Someone behind Lee was openly sobbing. Aunt Sally? Had to be. The priest turned away, signaling to everyone that the service was concluded and the gathered mourners turned away also. Then everyone froze as a screeching whine interrupted the pastoral silence. The electric winch chugged as a belt slipped, dipping the polished casket to one end where it tilted out of the grave like a ship going down. A number of uncles rushed forward, Lee's father included, and tried to reset the belt to right the angled casket. The attendant from the funeral home apologized profusely, assuring the mourners they would rectify the glitch immediately. The priest ushered everyone along, reminding all of the reception at the farmhouse later.

"Come along," said Lee's mother, slipping her hand through

his arm for balance as she negotiated the uneven terrain of the lawn. Lee glanced back over his shoulder to his grandmother's casket listing in its hole and the two men from the funeral home struggling to fix the winch. One last mourner lingered near the grave, a tall man in a dark suit who stood out among the others with his slicked pompadour hair and long sideburns. A rockabilly goon, long gone to seed. Plucking the pink carnation from his lapel, the man with the sideburns tossed the flower onto the coffin where it rolled from the polished lid into the darkness below.

———————— ✦◆✦ ————————

The farm was a ten-minute drive from the cemetery, beyond the outskirts of town where the landscape gave way to fallow fields that once yielded barley and corn and soy. The home of the late Marion Traven rose into view at the end of a long driveway flanked by elm trees, a faded clapboard house with a wraparound veranda that sagged at one end. A stand of cedar trees formed a windbreak on the north side of the property and beyond that rose the silhouette of a dilapidated barn.

Vehicles were lined along the gravel driveway and parked haphazardly over the front yard, the placards from the funeral home still wedged into the hood seams. Mourners made their way to the front door with trays of food or brown-bagged offerings from the liquor store. Lee's father cursed his own kin for ruining the grass as he rolled their truck to an empty spot near the old swing set. Lee climbed out and retrieved the cooler from the tailgate, looking over the decrepit swing he used to play on as a kid. With its rusting poles and corroded chains, the flimsy structure looked like a tetanus trap waiting to ensnare any youngster foolish enough to play on it.

"Hustle up," said his father, urging the family along toward the farmhouse. The screen door banged shut repeatedly as people in their Sunday best made their way inside. "Let's get this over with."

The sideboard in the dining room was cluttered with trays of cheese and cold cuts and tubs of potato salad. Nothing fancy, but lots of it. The adult fortifications had to be trucked in as Grandma Traven was a staunch believer in temperance who forbade a drop of the stuff in her house while she was alive. Bottles were slipped from the paper bags and plunked down onto the kitchen counter, the glass rattling as more bottles were added to their number. The house, with its worn-out furniture and faded wallpaper, was brimming with aunts in sleeved dresses and uncles unaccustomed to neckties. They spoke in hushed tones as they balanced paper plates on their knees or clinked ice into glasses. Children rampaged through the house until they were scolded to be quiet or shooed outdoors.

Squeezing through the mourners, Lee slipped free of his parents and made his way from the dining room to the parlor, searching the assembled clan for one face in particular. Aunt Sally was tucking a tissue into her sleeve and Uncle Bill was bragging about his boat, but there was no sign of her anywhere among the crowd. Lee felt someone tug his elbow.

"Lee," a man's voice said. Uncle Rob, reaching through the bodies to snag him. "How are you, son?"

"I'm all right," Lee replied. He nodded at the people pressed around them. "Packed house, huh?"

Rob nodded his head. "Shame we have to wait for a funeral to get the family together like this."

"Too bad Grandma Traven wasn't here to see this. She would have loved it."

"True. Except for this, of course." Uncle Rob raised his glass and took a sip. "She would have chased us all out with a broom."

Lee studied his glass with a covetous eye. He'd sneak one later when no one was looking. "Say, have you seen Zoe?"

"Isn't she still at school?"

"I guess, but I thought she'd be home for the funeral."

Uncle Rob looked over the room, shrugged and then turned back to his nephew. "Speaking of school, you hear back from college yet?"

"No," Lee lied. "Not yet."

The letter had arrived last week. It was sitting unopened on the desk in his bedroom. A thin envelope with a single page inside. There was no need to open it. If he'd been accepted, the envelope would have been thick with information pamphlets.

"I'm sure you'll hear back soon," his uncle said. He nodded at the food-laden sideboard across the room. "Better get yourself something to eat before it's all picked over. Grief makes people hungry."

He moved on, pressing through the crowd, trying not to upset anyone's plate of food or sloshing cocktail. From the den to the sunroom, he circled back to the dining room, eyes peeled but Zoe was nowhere to be found. The collective volume in the house was rising as the family grieved and gossiped and shared jokes that everyone had heard a million times before. Pushing through another tangle of elbows and gesturing hands, Lee inadvertently stepped into a circle of adults despairing about the details now that the funeral was over.

Aunt Sally, her cheeks flushed from tears, gestured to the cluttered shelves and side-tables around the room. "Look at all this stuff. When did mom become such a packrat?"

"It's been like this for a while, Sal," Aunt Pauline replied with no small amount of scorn. "When was the last time you were here?"

Sally ignored the remark, sweeping her gaze over the mismatched picture frames, ceramic figurines and greenglass bowls of dust-fuzzy mints. "What are we going to to do with it all? Just sorting through it is going to be a nightmare."

Lee's father was already on his second rye and Coke. Grant Traven gave a dismissive wave to the whole room. "Forget sorting this junk. We sell the place as is. Problem solved."

Lee watched Aunt Sally brighten at the notion but Aunt Pauline hardened her gaze at her younger brother. "Who says we're selling the farm?"

"What else are we gonna do with it?" his father asked, returning the withering look. "Are you going to work the farm?"

Pauline bit her tongue, glowering. Aunt Sally continued to pick through a shelf of knick-knacks. "As much as I hate the idea of it, maybe we should go through everything. There's antiques and heirlooms here."

"And how do we divide it up?" Pauline asked. "Mom didn't leave a will."

Brushing the dust from her hands, Sally said "We separate it into categories, then item-by-item. There's the furniture, the appliances, silverware, farm equipment and so on."

Grant sneered at the suggestion. "Farm equipment? That stuff hasn't been used since dad died. It's worthless now."

"I'm sure it's worth something," Sally replied.

"Itemizing everything will take forever."

Pauline's glower had not diminished. "Are you afraid of a little hard work, Grant? There isn't a quick-fix to everything, you know."

Their voices were becoming louder and more of the adults were crowding in to hear the exchange or add their two-cents. Sensing the row heating up, Lee began backing away when he felt a hand on his arm.

"Lee," said his father, "did you get the beer from the truck?"

Lee winced. "No."

"Well, go put it in the fridge before it gets warm."

Gladly. Pushing through the tattered screen door, he came out onto the front lawn to find the sun punishing down. He shook out of the suit jacket and stripped off the hated tie, tossing both into the pickup truck before opening the squeaky tailgate. The two cases of beer were hidden under the tarp to protect them from the sun and were, thankfully, still cool to the touch. If there was one surefire way to get on his old man's bad side, it was to let the beer get warm.

He was sliding the cases out when he heard a voice behind him.

"Hey."

Lee turned around to see the face that he'd been searching for earlier smiling back at him.

2

One cousin in particular - University life - Reminiscing - A quarrel and a vow - Uncle Elvis - Greed trumps all

ZOE SMILED AT HIM, her face shaded from the sun by a floppy hat that matched her black dress. The same smile that he always knew, the kind that squinted her eyes. She had a phantom dimple on her left cheek that would only appear when her smile brightened at full bloom. Lee didn't realize how much he had missed it until it made a faint flutter on her cheek before vanishing again.

"Hey back," he said. He could feel his own smile hurting his cheeks but felt unable to dial it down. "I wasn't sure if you'd be here."

"Of course, I'd be here," she said. "Grandma died."

Zoe came around the back of the pickup slowly, her heels wobbly on the gravel drive. Lee studied her, trying to pinpoint why she looked different now. Was it just the formal attire for the funeral or had something changed? Maybe first-year university did that to people, matured them into proper adults. Lee didn't know. And, according to the unopened letter on his desk, he never would.

Shielding his eyes from the sun, he said: "How was first year?"

"Fantastic," she said, her smile beaming brighter at the mention of it. "I didn't want to leave."

"Cool." He glanced over the yard of parked cars and the barn in the distance then back to her. Her dress was sleeveless and the tops of her shoulders were blushed pink. "You look a little sunburnt."

Zoe looked down at her bare shoulder. "I'm so pale right now. Finals were so tough I barely went outdoors the last few months of school. At least I'm not so freckly."

"Freckles aren't so bad." He dragged the beer cases to the lip of the tailgate and stacked one atop the other.

"You restocking the fridge?"

"Yeah," he said. "You wanna help?"

"Sure." She took hold of the top case and hauled it up.

"I can carry them," he protested.

"I got it, tough guy." Her heels were wobbly under the weight of the box but she nodded at him to carry on. As they went up the steps to the back door, she added: "Just like old times, huh?"

Setting their burdens on the scuffed floor of the kitchen, Zoe tore open the first box and passed the bottles forward as Lee stacked them into the outdated refrigerator.

"When did you get back?"

"Last night."

He looked at her. "You should have called. We coulda hung out."

"It was late," she said, handing across another pair of bottles. "I was tired."

"Oh."

The noise from the other room smothered them, a few voices rising louder than others in the crowded house. Lee watched his cousin peel off the floppy hat and fling it like a Frisbee onto the table.

"I saw your dad earlier," he said. "How's he doing?"

Zoe shrugged. "Hard to tell. Part of his face is still paralyzed. It's hard for him to talk, you know? Hard for him to do anything right now."

Lee nodded. "Must be hard on your mom."

"Yeah, she's working herself ragged looking after him and the business. Now I'm worried she'll have a stroke, too."

"Aunt Fran's pretty tough. I'm sure she'll be okay—"

A ruckus from the other room cut him off as Lee's father and Zoe's mother barged into the kitchen. They were still arguing about the farm.

"So what are you saying?" bellowed Lee's dad. "We get the assets and you get the property? Give me freaking break, Fran."

Zoe's mom planted her fists on her hips. "What's wrong with that? It's fair."

"The land is the only thing of real value here. Why the hell do you get most of it?"

Fran pointed a finger at her brother. "I'm the one who looked after Mom when she got sick. None of you bothered to help me."

Lee and Zoe shared a glance as more relations poured into the kitchen, carrying their disagreements with them like it was a traveling sideshow. None of them seemed to notice the pair crouched before the open Kelvinator.

Uncle Bill barged into the center of the room, almost crashing into Zoe. "We helped when we could, Fran," he shouted back. "And I appreciate what you did but that doesn't mean you get the lion's share."

Zoe winced as her mother's voice boomed over the kitchen. "Did you feed Mom when she couldn't do it herself? Were you here to help bathe her or treat her bedsores?" Fran wagged a finger at her two brothers. "No, you two stayed away, waiting for her to die!"

"That's not true and you know it," barked Lee's dad. "You always gotta be the martyr, don't you?"

Now it was Lee's turn to wince and feel his cheeks burn with shame at his father's outburst. The tension inside their grandmother's kitchen stretched taut as the skin of a drum. Then Aunt Sally, the youngest of the squabbling siblings, burst into the room and pleaded for them all to stop yelling. Her eyes were red and her voice cracked. Zoe's mother stormed out of the room and the others followed, taking the fight with them as if determined to poison every room in the house with it.

Lee leaned back against the cold fridge and heard Zoe expel a long sigh as if she'd been holding her breath. Neither spoke for a moment, unwilling to break the spell of a quiet room and then Zoe plucked two more bottles from the case on the floor and handed them to him.

"Jesus Christ," she wheezed. "Grandma's not even cold in the ground and they're already fighting over who gets what."

Lee shook his head. "Did you hear my old man? Every time I think he can't stoop any lower, he manages to drop a rung or two."

"It's pathetic," Zoe agreed.

A third voice broke behind them, startling them both.

"Money and family don't mix."

Zoe and Lee whipped around to see a man seated at the kitchen table, his boots propped up on an empty chair like he owned the place. There was gray peppered in his long sideburns and ghostly strands of it running through his slick-backed hair. A garish belt buckle, like the kind truck drivers wore, sparkled under the dip of his pink shirt. The same man that Lee had seen toss a carnation into the open grave of Grandma Traven. His name was Eddie, or maybe Teddy. No one was really sure. To everyone in the family, he was simply Uncle Elvis.

Lee regarded the man with his grin and feet up on the chair. He had never liked Uncle Elvis and usually avoided him at any family function. "What's that supposed to mean?"

Uncle Elvis just grinned. "Grief does funny things to people. Makes 'em ugly."

Zoe looked away. Like her cousin, she had never been fond of this uncle with his rockabilly look and off-color jokes. "How can they squabble over money at a time like this?"

"Par for the course, darling." Uncle Elvis dropped his boots to the floor with a thud and rose to his feet. "Blood may be thicker than water, but greed? Well, greed trumps all."

Lee sneered at the sentiment. "You'd never catch me acting that low. Jesus."

Laughter bubbled out of Uncle Elvis like he'd never heard anything so funny. And then he reached out and took the beer from Zoe's hand. "You're a funny kid, you know that?"

He stepped over the two of them, clomping his heavy boots on the floor as he did so. He ruffled Lee's hair before sauntering out the back door, still chuckling.

Zoe turned to her cousin. "Is it just me or does Uncle Elvis get creepier every year?"

Lee's grin was short-lived as the cacophony of voices bellowed from the other room. The bickering between the parental units had lost none of its steam and, given its growing volume, it was heading back toward the kitchen.

Lee took two bottles and handed one to her. "You wanna get outta here?"

3

Empty stalls and long-dead horses - Barn kittens - The short career of a reformed arsonist - The workshop - Strange instruments and a map - The Buccaneer 2000 - Chastised by the King

THE BARN HAD always been a refuge for the youngest of each successive generation; a place to escape to within its dust mottled air and phantom odor of livestock. The bay door creaked on its ancient hinges as the cousins stepped into the gloomy interior. The horse stalls stood empty, the bars shrouded in cobwebs. Moldering hay lay strewn over the cobbled floor and the hulk of a derelict Massey Ferguson squatted near the rear bay like a sleeping giant.

Sunlight winked through the numerous gaps in the barn walls and Lee stepped into the solid shafts of dust-roiling light.

"You home for the summer or just the funeral?"

"The summer," Zoe replied, crossing to one of the empty stalls.

"Maybe longer."

Lee turned around, surprised at the remark. He tempered his enthusiasm. "Longer? Aren't you going back to school in the fall?"

"Dunno. With dad's stroke, mom's run a bit ragged. I can't just abandon her and run back to school, can I?"

"Aunt Fran won't stand for that. Or she'd never admit she can't do it."

Zoe surveyed the abandoned stalls. Dessicated straw lay piled in one corner, giving off a slightly combustible odor. The water trough tilted toward the ground, hanging on by one last bolt. The whole thing looked forlorn. "I used to love coming here when we were kids. Do you remember when Grandpa kept horses?"

Grandpa John had worked the farm long after he should have, refusing to let any of his sons take over. Not that any of them had wanted to, but that was beside the point. He had kept a few horses right up to the end; a big Belgian draft and an American Paint.

"I remember the big draft that used to kick the stalls," Lee said. "Scared the hell out of me."

She laughed. "He only did that when you were around."

"Lucky me."

He watched her pass out of the stall to the rough-milled ladder on the post. She looked up at the dark monk-hole leading to the hayloft above.

"Do you remember haying season?" she asked, eyes alight with nostalgia. "The two of us up there dying in the heat and the dust, catching bales from the conveyor belt."

"I remember the welts we'd get from all that straw."

Zoe laughed at the memory, almost feeling the prickly sensation of hard straw needling her forearms. She kicked at the straw on the floor, billowing more dust into the stagnant barn air. "They're gonna sell this place as soon as they can, aren't they?"

Lee tugged at a gunny rope hanging from an overhead beam. "What else are they going to do with it?"

The inevitability of it settled over them like a foregone conclusion, the loss of this childhood refuge with its stifling heat and animal musk.

Zoe gathered her hair up onto her head to cool the back of her neck. She looked at her cousin. "You keeping out of trouble?"

"What else am I gonna do? Things are boring as hell around here."

"They were boring before," she said.

"It's worse now."

Something small and gray darted out of one of the stalls. A mangy kitten bounding over the hay, circling her ankle. Zoe squealed with delight and bent down to gather it up, curling it onto her collarbone. "Poor kitty," she cooed to the damp-eyed kitten. "Who's gonna feed you now that Grandma's gone?"

Lee studied her as she tilted her chin down onto the clotted fur of the kitten's head.

She caught him staring, her brow knitting in faux surprise. "What?" she said.

"Nothing," he replied and looked away.

A thud rang through the vast space of the barn, causing a

swallow to sail from its nest and flit through the rafter beams.

"What was that?"

Another thud, this time from the far end where the door to the workshop was closed. As they crept toward it, the low murmur of voices could be heard coming from behind it. Lee turned the knob and pushed the door open.

Like the rest of the barn, the workshop was gloomy and still like a sealed tomb. The lathe and band saw lay frosted with sawdust, the workbenches neglected and forgotten. Wooden chairs hung from the ceiling waiting for a repair that would never happen.

The only thing moving inside the gloomy space were two young men passing a joint between them. Like Lee, both were dressed in the suits they had worn to the prom. More cousins from the funeral.

"Close the door already," said the bigger one. Jeremy. A year younger than Lee but a foot taller with a hundred more pounds of solid muscle. A natural athlete who excelled at every sport, Jeremy was almost the polar opposite to Lee.

Zoe scooted in alongside Lee and closed the door behind them. "What are you guys doing in here?"

"Same as you," said the other one. "Getting away from the parental units."

This was Truman. Two years older than Lee and three times more trouble. Truman was the one who came up with stupid, sometimes dangerous stunts that often led to catastrophe. Egging cars on the highway or setting off strings of firecrackers on a neighbor's porch. All good fun but when Truman went through his arsonist phase, Lee began to distance himself. Garden sheds had gone up in flames, dumpster bins became foul-smelling infernos. The pinnacle of that arsonist summer had been an abandoned house down near the river. The property had stood empty for years until one night when it all went up in a fire that was visible across town. No one was ever charged and Truman denied any involvement but Lee knew the truth. The sheer scale of the destruction must have scared even Truman, for there were no more mysterious fires after that.

The other thing about cousin Truman was that he was forever injured, constantly on the mend from a broken bone or a nasty wound. Even now his left arm was clad in a cast from elbow to wrist but the cause of the injury, like always, remained shrouded in mystery. He was reckless and had little regard for consequences.

"The harpies were turning shrill in there," Truman said, wielding a hacksaw. Clamping a shotgun shell to the bench vise, he was halfway through sawing open the plastic shell casing. Buckshot and powder spilled over the crusty workbench. "Jeremy was about to cry so I brought him out here."

"Fuck you," Jeremy spat. Moving in on the intruders, he snatched the beer out of Lee's hand. "Gimme that."

"Get your own."

"Pipe down, short-stuff." Jeremy pushed him away and tilted back the bottle, glugging it down.

Zoe rolled her eyes at the brutishness of her cousins. It was nothing new to her. "Don't be such a goon, Jeremy."

The muscled teen dried pretend tears. "Zoe, you hurt my feelings."

Sweeping the gunpowder into a tidy pile, Truman turned to Lee. "What's with your old man? Dude's yelling at everybody."

"They're already fighting over the farm," Lee answered.

Jeremy sneered at him. "Why does he have to be such an asshole? He made my mom cry."

"Please," Zoe said with an equal amount of scorn. "Your mom cries over everything."

When Truman laughed Jeremy told him to shut up but the cousin with the cast threw gunpowder at him.

Zoe placed a fingertip to the coat of sawdust on the lathe and spelled her name. "Did either of you see Grandma before she died?"

Truman shrugged. "Not since Thanksgiving."

"I saw her at Christmas," Jeremy said. "She looked pretty frail."

Lee toured the machines of the workshop, all of them idle since their grandfather had passed years ago. Before that, none of them had ever been allowed inside. For Lee, it was like breaking into a Pharaoh's tomb, an inner sanctum of mysteries and secrets. He was drawn to the far corner where the greasy light from the window didn't reach. Unlike the other areas of the shop, the workbench here was covered by a stained drop cloth. Folding it back he uncovered an array of tools, books, and maps. There were two spades and a pick-ax, a small trowel, and a straw whisk. The yellowed pages of the notebooks were filled with chicken scratch and Lee lost interest when he could not decipher the cramped penmanship. Drawing his attention more was the odd-looking instrument at the back of the bench; a long pole with a grip on one end and a disk on the other. The logo on the shaft read *Buccaneer Pro 2000.*

Why did Grandpa have a metal detector?

Behind him, Truman was carrying on. Bored with the gunpowder, he snapped a lighter and re-lit the joint. "Take a good look around, folks," he said. "We won't be seeing this place again."

"That really sucks," Zoe sighed. "I love the farm."

Jeremy spat onto the sawdust floor. "Why can't they just leave it alone?"

"Because," Truman pronounced, "they all think they're owed something."

"Like what?"

Truman shrugged. "Ask them."

Ignoring the banter, Lee hoisted up the metal detector and inspected the control panel near the molded handle. Gripping it fast, he switched it on and waved the sensor disk over an iron bench vise. The resultant squeal of the finder stung everyone's ears.

"The fuck are you doing, Lee?"

"Sorry," he said, setting the Buccaneer 2000 back onto the workbench.

Zoe came up alongside him. "What is all this?"

"Grandpa's old stuff."

"What's with all the maps?" She rifled through a stack of the maps, unfolding a few at a time. "Check it out. This one's a topographical map. And a land survey map. Weird."

"And this one," Lee said, nodding at another map pinned to the wall over the workbench. A property map that had been scribed with a grid over one section of land. Dozens of tiny boxes marked with an X through them. "What's with all these squares?"

"It's the farm," she said, pointing at the landmarks of the farmhouse and the barn. "See the road here? And the house and barn. Looks like Grandpa divided the entire property on this grid system."

"What for?" asked Truman, moving in for a closer look.

"Who knows," Zoe said. "Maybe he was planning on selling off parcels of land."

All four of them poked through the clutter on the workbench. Jeremy unlatched a wooden box to find an antique transit and compass while Zoe unfurled another map. Truman took up the metal detector while Lee rummaged a stack of moldering books, scanning titles like *Archeology for Beginners* and *Jesse James was his Name.*

"Weird collection of books," Truman said. Putting aside the Buccaneer, he checked the titles on the spines. "The Outlaw Jesse James, A History of Shackleton, Confederate Gold."

"Boring," Jeremy said. "Where's Grandpa's stash of titty mags?"

"Your mom burned them all," said Zoe.

Lee unearthed a cigar box from underneath a stack of newspapers and flipped open the lid to reveal a collection of metal artifacts. Oversize pennies of oxidized copper, rusted clasps and buckles, two antique bullets, a spur and, buried at the bottom, a heavy coin. Wiping the dirt off with his thumb, the metal beneath gleamed in the weak light.

He showed it to Zoe. "That look like gold to you?"

"Dunno. Looks kind of dull to be gold. Is there a date on it?"

Wetting his thumb, Lee began working the grime away when a gruff voice startled them all.

"The hell're you doing in here?"

They spun around, looking guilty as hell to find Uncle Elvis standing in the doorway.

"Nothing," answered Truman.

"Bullshit." The older man stomped forward, his boot heels ringing off the stones. He snatched the coin from Lee's hands. "You thieves pilfering your grandfather's stuff?"

"We were just looking around," Lee protested.

"Out." Elvis tossed the coin back into the cigar box and closed the lid. "All of you."

Jeremy, who had never liked their eccentric uncle, was already out the door. Zoe lingered, nodding at the equipment on the workbench. "What is all this stuff?"

"Junk. Your Grandpa had some peculiar hobbies. C'mon, everybody out."

They turned to follow Jeremy out the door. As they passed, the older man cuffed Truman across the back of the head. "Don't smoke weed in here, dummy. You'll burn the damn barn down."

Truman held his tongue but his eyes registered pure murder before disappearing from the room. Lee took a last look back as he went out the door to see Uncle Elvis drape the drop cloth back over the bench.

4

**Father and son - The fate of the farm - An old man's hobbies
- Family folklore - The lost treasure of a notorious outlaw**

THE WAKE AT the farm ended in acrimony as the bickering
continued and everyone stormed out to their vehicles. Insisting
that Lee's father was in no shape to drive, his mother drove the
truck home despite the fact that she too would have failed a
breathalyzer test had they been pulled over by the police. But
there was little chance of that as Carthage had one police station
with few officers and the streets were often quiet after sundown.

Returning home, his mother announced that she was going to
bed and left the two of them in the kitchen. Lee scrounged up a
soda from the fridge and watched his father pour another drink.

"Dad, you sure you want another one?"

His father kept pouring. "Did you bury your mother today?"

Under normal circumstances, Lee would have simply retreated
to the basement den, but he lingered in the kitchen while his

father sipped rye and soda and gazed out the window.

"What's going to happen to the farm?"

His father shrugged as if the answer couldn't be more obvious. "It'll be sold."

"Can't we keep it?"

"No point. Sooner it's sold, the sooner we can settle everything."

Lee scratched his head. "But it's been in the family since forever. Doesn't that count for something?"

"Sentiment is nice, but it doesn't pay the back taxes." Grant Traven rubbed the back of his neck, tilting his head side to side to work out a kink. "You better get some sleep. You're opening the shop tomorrow."

The shop was the town arena, which his family owned, and where Lee had worked since he was twelve. The thought of putting in another dreary day there soured his guts. He turned to leave but then stopped and looked at his old man again.

"Dad?"

"Yeah."

"Did Grandpa have any hobbies?"

A crease formed on his father's brow. "He liked to play the ponies."

"I found a metal detector and some maps in the barn. A bunch of weird tools."

"That?" The older man chuckled and shook his head. "You're grandpa had some crazy notions."

"About what? Was he into cowboy history and stuff? Why all

the books about Jesse James?"

"According to your grandfather, he was family."

Lee almost laughed. "Get outta here."

"Haven't you heard that old story?" When his son shrugged, Grant Traven wiped the back of his hand across his mouth and went on. "Jesse James hid out here for a spell back in eighteen-whatever. The law is hot on his trail, see? So Jesse rides due north, slips across the border and comes here where, according to folklore, he's got relations that hide him."

Lee felt his jaw dropping. "For real?"

"No," his father said, waving the notion away with his hand. "It's all bullshit. But your grandfather believed it. Hell, he was was obsessed with it. Jesse James and his lost treasure."

"Lost what?" Lee cocked an ear toward his father, unsure of what he'd heard.

"Saddlebags full of money he'd stole from the banks and whatnot. According to the story, he buries it somewhere on the Traven farm to keep it safe until he can return with his family. But he never makes it back."

The kitchen was suddenly silent and Lee exhaled, unaware that he had been holding his breath.

His father finished his drink and rose from his chair, gripping the table to steady himself.

"Your grandfather was a tad bonkers, to put it mildly. He believed that story was real. Spent every spare moment looking for the damn thing." His father rose from the chair and put his empty glass into the sink. "Turn off the lights before you go to bed," he added as he left the room.

5

The stroke - Higher learning - Familial obligations - Quaking hands and spilled tea - Dashed hopes

WHEN THE KETTLE whistled, Zoe made tea and brought the pot to the table where her parents sat. They were all exhausted from the funeral and reception at the farm and all Zoe wanted to do was to crash onto the bed she hadn't slept in since Christmas but her mom insisted they all have some tea to unwind. She was still fuming over the encounter with her siblings, filling in every detail to Zoe about how selfish they all were.

"And then," she went on, "your uncle Bill claimed that the sideboard belonged to him because your grandmother had promised it to him. It's mahogany, you know. Conveniently, when no one else was around to confirm it. Can you believe that?"

Zoe spooned sugar and milk into her tea. She had learned to take it clear while at school but the day had been long and she wanted something comforting, so she mixed it how she used to take it as a kid; sweet and milky.

"It's still raw," she said to her mom. "The loss, the stress of arranging the funeral. Seeing her buried. Everyone's nerves are fried. I'm sure it was just stress and grief talking."

Her mother's lips pursed tightly. "That wasn't grief on display today, that was pure selfishness. I've seen it before. There's something about death that just brings out the worst in people."

Zoe reached across the table to pat her mother's hand. "Why don't we call it a day and see what tomorrow brings."

Her father had sat silently throughout this exchange, both hands wrapped around his steaming teacup. He raised the cup to his lips but his arm trembled and the tea sloshed down his shirt and onto his crotch. Catapulting into action, her mother reached for the dish towel while Zoe scooped the cup from his hand.

A look of frustration and shame darkened her father's face and Zoe averted her eyes, telling him everything was okay. She turned to her mother. "You said he was getting better?"

"He is," her mother stated flatly, blotting the tea from his shirt. "Two weeks ago he couldn't have even lifted the cup."

"It's been a month since the stroke. He doesn't seem all that better to me."

"The doctor made no promises," her mother replied, fetching a straw from the drawer.

Zoe straightened her back. "How's the business? Can Brendan handle the work?"

Her mother folded the damp towel and laid it on the table. "He's trying but without your father there, he can only do so much."

Zoe stirred her tea. Her father was an electrician with one employee, a lad named Brendan who had started working this spring. Brendan could do the grunt work but without her father on the job site, the work would stall and future jobs would have to be postponed, if not canceled outright.

"I don't know what we're going to do," her mother sighed wearily. "We can't get by on my salary alone and if your father's recovery is long term, the business will close up."

Zoe offered her mom a smile but she was tired and it felt forced. "We'll figure it out. And Dad will get better. I know he will."

"I'm glad you're home," her mother replied.

"Me too."

Her mom wiped her eyes and raised her teacup. "Someone needs to be with your dad at all times now. Between the two of us, we can manage but we need to tighten our belts for the time being and pinch every penny."

"Of course. We have the summer. Plenty of time to figure it out before I go back to school."

Her mother tried to rouse a brave face but the smile she offered was tight-lipped. And then she uttered a phrase that, in Zoe's experience, often forewarned negative results. "We'll see," she said.

6

Ice time - An unhappy coach – Carthage Coyotes - Orange bile - Wunderkind - A request - Rumors of a bonfire

THE ARENA WAS kept open until mid-June when it became too costly to maintain the ice in the summer heat. Lee arrived early to open the place up and prep the ice for the Carthage Coyotes, the town's junior hockey league. Jeremy was among the cluster of players already waiting outside at dawn to be let in.

Lee apologized to the hulking young men crowding around as he fumbled with the keys. "Sorry, guys. Just gimme a minute, okay?"

"You're late," complained Jeremy.

"By two minutes," Lee said, throwing open the door.

"That's two minutes of lost ice time," replied Stanfield, the Shark's coach. "That's two minutes we paid for but didn't get, son. These boys need to warm up."

Lee rushed to turn on the floodlights. "You can get your two minutes at the end, Mr. Stanfield."

Stanfield was a blowhard who insisted on having the last word in every conversation. "But those two minutes cut into the figure skating time after us. They're not going to like that either."

"Yeah, but they're not armed with sticks, are they?"

Stanfield shook his head. "No, what they got is moms. You get on the wrong side of the skate-moms, you're in for a world of hurt."

Lee ignored the remark but his cousin jostled him with his hockey bag as he sauntered to the change room. "Just be on time, fucknuts," Jeremy said.

Later that morning, as the Carthage Coyotes roared across the rink and slammed one another into the boards, Lee took out his phone and dialed a number. He listened to it ring three times before she picked up.

"Hello?"

"Hey," Lee said. "What're you up to?"

"Helping out with dad," Zoe replied. "Are you at work?"

Lee moved away from the noise of the rink and crossed into the lobby. "Yeah. Jeremy and his buddies are murdering each other on the ice."

"Some things never change, huh?"

"Not here," he said, looking over the drab lobby with its cinderblock walls and display cases of forgotten trophies. "Nothing ever changes here."

There was a pause before she spoke. "So what's up?"

"Do you want to hang out later? We could go down to the river if you want."

There was another pause. "I got stuff to do."

"Oh," he said. "We can meet after you're done. I mean, if you want."

"I can't. There's just too much to do around here with Dad and stuff. You know?"

"Sure."

"Maybe later in the week?"

"Okay. See ya." He hung up without waiting for a reply, feeling foolish and needy, but his mind was already mitigating it with excuses. She just got home. She's got a lot on her plate. Especially since Uncle Don's stroke.

Feeling a tug on his arm, he turned to find a little girl in a sparkling outfit looking up at him. One of the figure skaters, waiting for the Sharks to get off the ice.

"Yeah?"

The girl pointed to the bleachers on the far side of the rink. "Someone barfed in the blue seats."

A large splatter of orange vomit waited for him on the concrete floor of the stands. Feeling his own stomach curdle at the smell of it, Lee held his breath as he began scraping the chunky mess into a dustpan. On the ice behind him, the Sharks rammed into the boards as they chased the puck. Jeremy glided past and, seeing Lee bent to his task, laughed at him.

He dumped the wretched mess into a bucket. This is your life, he mused. Mopping up someone's puke while the hockey hero skates a victory lap. A nightmarish image came to him just then, flash-forwarding to the future where he saw himself years from now, still mopping up vomit, still stuck in this armpit of a town. The pungent reek, disturbed by the pan, overwhelmed him. Lee dropped the dustpan and stepped away trying to keep his stomach down.

He thought back to the crazy story his father had told him, about his grandfather digging for buried treasure. Like the stories about Bigfoot and UFOs, he knew it was nonsense but he kept circling back to it all morning. The maps and tools in the barn spoke to how seriously his grandfather had taken the Jesse James story. It was ludicrous he knew, but it begged a question difficult to dismiss. What if it was true?

"Is this mess gonna clean itself?" his father's voice boomed out of nowhere. He frowned in disgust at the foul-smelling bucket.

"The smell got to me," Lee said, reaching for the dustpan. "I was afraid I was going to add to it."

"All the more reason to get it out of sight," his father said. A flash of blue and gold raced by the plexiglass as Jeremy and his teammates roared across the blue line. Grant Traven moved closer to the boards and watched the Sharks practice. "Jesus," he said with admiration. "Look at that kid skate."

Lee didn't ask who he was referring to. He didn't need to.

"Your cousin's got real talent," his father said. "What's more, he's got focus and discipline. That'll take him far."

Lee tilted the dustpan, letting the orange bile drip into the bucket. "He's a real wunderkind."

"You could learn a thing or two about focus from him."

"I could also learn to be an obnoxious asshole, too."

Grant Traven regarded his son with a slow shake of his head. "That's just being petty."

"Can I borrow the truck tonight?"

His father turned back to watch the action on the ice. "Not a chance."

"Why not?"

"Do I look stupid to you? I know there's a bonfire tonight. You think I'm going to let you have the truck to get trashed?"

Lee looked up from the vomit and frowned. Bonfire parties were a semi-regular event during the summer. The location was kept secret until the day of, to keep the police from showing up too soon. Lee was a little dismayed to learn that his father knew of the upcoming bonfire party before he did.

"That's not what I want it for."

Keeping his attention on the ice, his father shook his head again. "I don't want you anywhere near that party. You need to steer clear of that stuff, keep your head straight. It's bad enough you failed last year."

"I didn't fail," Lee countered. "I just didn't get into college."

This time his father turned and looked directly at him.

"Is there a difference?"

7

Library - Dune - The spartan shelf of the History section - An empty playground - Hitching a ride - The farm under starlight

THE CARTHAGE PUBLIC Library was small, under-stocked and smelled of cheap air freshener. Locking the doors to the arena after work, Lee had hurried across town on his bike to slip inside before the library closed. Aside from the librarian, the only people inside were two frumpy-looking men sitting slumped before the outdated computer terminals, their faces lit up in the glare of the dusty screens.

There was nothing new in the science-fiction/fantasy stacks, or even the mystery section. The same titles leered back at him with their smudgy covers and wrinkled spines. Out of desperation, he grabbed a dog-eared copy of *Dune*, even though he'd read it before, and then moved further down the stacks.

The history section was scant and what it did have was old. Lee rummaged through a few books on American history, particularly the Civil War era, but found no reference to the famous bank robber in its indexes. The only thing he could find on Jesse James was a chapter in a children's book about the Old West. He took it anyway.

Gliding the bike back along the main drag, he stopped at Gino's for a slice and rode on to the town square. A tall cenotaph stood as the centerpiece of the small square and he took a seat at its base, bit into the greasy pizza and read the chapter on Jesse James. It was a simplified overview of his role as an irregular in the Civil War, his disillusionment at the defeat of the Confederacy and his exploits robbing banks with his brother Frank. His life ended with a bullet to the back of the head from one of his own gang members. The chapter concluded with an archly romantic allusion to the outlaw as an American Robin Hood, stealing from the rich carpetbaggers of the era and giving to the poor.

Putting the book aside he opened the Dune paperback and skimmed through the first three pages but closed it again, feeling unsatisfied and still hungry. Looking across the square, he surveyed the main street of town, all but deserted at this hour. A car rode south, a pickup truck rumbled in the opposite direction and then a dark Volvo station wagon appeared and parked before the liquor store. Aunt Fran's station wagon. When he saw Zoe climb out and run into the store, he quickly stuffed the books into his backpack and reached for his bike.

Reemerging from the liquor store, Zoe was surprised to find her cousin leaning up against the Volvo's fender.

"Hey," she said.

"What are you doing?"

She held up the paper bag and, with a mocking tone, said: "Buying shoes?"

"You're going to the bonfire party?"

"Yeah. You?"

"I don't even know where it is," he said.

Coming around the car, she opened the hatch and dropped the bag inside. "It's at the wind field."

"Again? They must be running out of places to have it." Lee looked up at a faultless sky of stars and then back to her. "You want to go for a drive?"

"I can't," she said. "I'm meeting Cynthia and Moira there. And I'm the one bringing the cocktails."

She was about to close the hatch but he stopped her and hoisted his bike into the back. "I need a ride out to the farm. It's on the way."

"I'm already running late."

"It won't take long. Come on, there's something I want to show you."

The road was a gray ribbon of asphalt lit up in the headlights, flanked on both sides with dark fields of new corn stalks. The radio chattered with a jangly pop song as the breeze rippled through the open window. Lee stole a glance at the driver. One hand on the wheel, the other propped up in the window, her features lit dimly by the dashboard lights. The cloying pop tune ended. Lee fidgeted in his seat, restless.

"How's your dad?"

She shrugged. "Mom says he's improving but I don't see it."

"I tried to talk to him at the farmhouse but I couldn't make out what he was saying."

"It's hard for him," she replied. "Part of his face is still seized up."

"He looked frustrated."

"He is."

The music faded, replaced by the mindless chatter of an obnoxious DJ. Zoe reached out to lower the volume. He thought she was going to continue but she just drove on.

"Have you been by the old drive-in?"

She shook her head. "I heard it's being torn down?"

"It is."

The Starlight Drive-In was a holdover from another era, closed down before either of them was born. It sat untouched since then, slowly being reclaimed by nature. Stalks of timothy grew around the speaker posts and creeping vine had snaked its way up the broad expanse of the screen. The concession stand had begun to sink slowly into the ground. The two of them had spent countless lazy summer days exploring the drive-in, projecting imaginary movies onto the tattered screen.

"Some land developer bought it up," he informed her. "They're gonna bulldoze the whole thing."

"That's a shame. We used to have so much fun there."

His hopes brightened. "We should go back one last time.

Before it's gone forever."

"Maybe," she replied, sounding noncommittal. Then she nodded at something up ahead. "We're here."

Gravel crunched under the tires as they turned onto the long driveway of the farm. The clapboard house flashed up in the sweep of the headlights as the car trundled past it to the barn. Zoe killed the engine and darkness swallowed the barn, the fields, everything.

"Leave the headlights on," he said.

"That'll drain the battery."

"We won't be that long. Come on."

They climbed out and approached the bay doors. Zoe pointed at the tiny pinpricks of light throbbing around them.

"Fireflies," she said.

"Maybe we can find a mason jar and catch a few."

Throwing back the latch, he swung the door wide and disappeared inside. A dusty lightbulb popped on. She followed him across the uneven stone floor to the workshop at the far end.

"So? What's so important?"

"This," he said, unfurling the drop cloth from the workbench. Zoe looked over the dusty tools and yellowing maps, unimpressed.

"You dragged me out here for this?"

Lee scrounged through the books on the bench and piled up three of them. "You heard of Jesse James?"

"The guy on TV who makes hot-rods?"

"The other one. The bank robber guy." He watched her open the cover of one of the books and flip through the pages. "Did you know you're related to him? And that he hid out here for a while on the farm?"

He had hoped for a shocked reaction. What he got was an eye-roll.

"Who told you that one? Uncle Frank?"

Ignoring the taunt, he went on. "He brings with him saddlebags full of gold and buries them somewhere out on the farm. This farm."

"Please..." she replied.

He passed a hand over the bench. "That's what all this stuff is for. The metal detector, the maps, shovels. Grandpa was looking for it."

"Grandpa went a little dotty in his golden years. Remember?"

"Look, I'll show you." Rooting up the old cigar box, he rifled through the metal debris for the coin he had seen earlier. Not finding it, he dumped the contents onto the bench. "It's gone."

Zoe was already moving to the door. "I gotta go."

"There was a gold coin here. An old one. I swear."

"I'm already late," she said, slipping out of the workshop. "Are you riding home or coming to the bonfire?"

Lee scavenged the metal artifacts again but still, no coin appeared. Gathering up the dusty volumes, he stuffed them into his backpack, along with one of the notebooks. As the car horn honked for him to hurry, he looked up at the map pinned over the bench with its strange grid penciled over it. Ripping it from the wall, he jammed it into his bag and ran to catch his ride.

8

**The turbines - Night fire - Tribes - A fan club - All-terrain
vehicle - Indiana Jones - A property map**

THE WIND FIELD was three miles out of town on the Old Cut
Road where eight giant wind turbines rose four hundred feet into
the night sky. The mammoth white blades turned slowly in their
hypnotic rotation against the shy winds coming off the open
plain. At the base of the most easterly turbine blazed the bonfire,
licking tendrils of flame into the ink black sky. Vehicles were
parked all over the uneven ground and the party-goers passed
before the fire like the tribe of some neolithic clan, shouting and
whooping odd war cries in an unintelligible tongue.

Zoe wedged the Volvo beside a Ram pickup with a bumper
sticker that read: *Don't like this country, feel free to leave it!*

"Half the town is here," Zoe said as they approached the
revelers. The heat of the fire rolled over them as they pressed
through the crowd. Shirtless young men hooted and egged each

other on to dive over the flames. One tumbled into the fire and rolled in a panic with his jeans alight. The others laughed and jeered at him.

"Christ," Zoe exclaimed. "What is about a fire that brings out the Neanderthal in dudes?"

Lee scanned the mob of his peers as they pumped their fists into the air and thumped their chests, all bluster and primate posturing. "It's like a pissing match, to see who can out-party everyone else. These losers are doomed to this backwater and they don't even know it."

"I'm so glad I brought you, Mister Cheerful," Zoe sneered back.

"You know what the funny part is?"

"What's that?"

"I'm no better off," he said. "Trapped here like all the rest."

She tilted her head to one side. "It's not so terrible, you know. This place."

"Easy for you to say. You got out."

"Yeah, well," she said, looking over the crush of sweating faces, "it's not all Vicodin and roses, you know."

He wasn't buying it. "Come on. This is all quaint nostalgia for you. Come September, you're gone."

She took the bag from him and plucked out a can of lager. "Don't be so sure about that."

"What does that mean?"

She cracked the tab and took a healthy pull on the beer. "Are you gonna buzzkill the whole night or can we go mingle?"

"Spot me a beer?"

"Mooch," she said as she thrust a can into his hand.

He watched her for a moment, seeing the ripple of the flames flash in her eyes, and tried to push words out of his mouth but his tongue felt numb so he dampened it with beer. Then a shriek broke out behind him as three girls from his class swarmed over his cousin.

"Zoe!" cried one, a do-gooder type named Melissa. "I heard you were back!"

"Why didn't you call?" whined another, her voice crackling with vocal-fry. "We missed you!"

Lee took a step back as Zoe was smothered in a huddle of old friends. Warm embraces and joyous smiles, the fan club pulled Zoe away, eager to catch up and trade war stories.

Abandoned, Lee looked over the faces of the crowd but could see not a friend among them. Within minutes he was wall-flowering on the periphery of the bonfire, trying hard not to look out of place.

He tried to remember if Zoe had locked her mom's station wagon. He wanted to get his bike and just slip away. A three-mile ride back into town but it was better than dying a slow death here. Draining his beer, he tossed the can into the fire and turned to go. Headlights flashed up hard in his eyes, a vehicle gunning right for him on a collision course. He leaped aside to avoid getting creamed, landing hard in the dry-choked earth.

The roar died as the engine was killed. Lee looked up to see a red Suzuki all-terrain vehicle with grime splattered mud flaps. The driver looked at him and pushed the helmet from his sweaty head. Jeremy regarded his cousin and chucked back his head with laughter.

Lee shot to his feet, brushing the dirt from his palms. "Real funny, Jay."

"Just messing with you, cuz," Jeremy laughed. "I'm surprised to see you here."

"Why is that?" Lee asked, trying to pull together some semblance of self-respect.

"Didn't you get the memo? No glee club allowed." He laughed again, unstrapping his case of beer from the rear cargo rack.

Lee cast a scornful eye on the case of Coors Light. "The beer of cowards, I see. I hope you brought enough for the whole class."

Jeremy peeled off the jacket that matched the red shell of his four-by-four. His biceps popped against the light of the bonfire. "See, that's your problem right there, Lee. You think you're being clever when you're just being a dick. You better run home before mom notices her baby is missing."

A roar went up from the crowd as someone chucked gasoline onto the fire, erupting the flames high into the night sky. Zoe took a step back from the rippling heat and bumped into Truman.

"Did you do that?" she asked, seeing the wide grin on his face.

"Not me," he replied, his eyes entranced by the blaze. "That would be dangerous."

"One of these days, Truman, you're gonna go too far."

"Hey," he said, wagging his chin at someone across the bonfire, "what's with the charity work?"

Lee stood alone amongst the party people, talking to no one.

"Don't be hard on him."

"I saw you guys pull up. What were you doing?"

"We stopped by the farm," she said, scanning the crowd for her groupies. "Lee wanted to root around in the barn."

Truman tore his eyes from the flames to look at her. "What for?"

"I don't know. Lee's geeking on some Indiana Jones thing."

The fan club reappeared, pulling Zoe away as they shot dagger glances at Truman.

"Why are you talking to that reprobate?" one asked.

Truman snatched Zoe's arm, holding her still. "What Indiana Jones thing?"

"I don't know," she called back as her friends carried her along. "Digging for pirate treasure or something."

He watched her disappear into the throng before turning back to where the cousin in question was wall-flowering on the periphery of the bonfire, but Lee had vanished.

The ride home left Lee sweaty and winded as he wheeled the bike into the garage. Creeping into the house, he saw a blue light churning against the living room walls. His father, asleep on the easy chair, snored softly against the blathering of the television. Lee plucked the remote from the coffee table, killed the TV, and crept on to his room.

Emptying the loot from the backpack onto his bed, he flipped through one of the battered paperbacks, stopping only to scan the tintypes. Tossing these aside, he opened the notebook and tried to decipher the cramped handwriting but gave up after a few pages. Saving the best for last, he unfolded the big map that he'd ripped from the barn wall and laid it flat.

The stamp on the property map was dated 1993 and the larger typeface read Belridge County. The lots of and concession were clearly marked and numbered, the roads and creek clearly illustrated. A heavy border of red marker had been traced around the entire perimeter of the Traven family farm and within this red border, a grid had been penciled in over the property. Each square of the grid was numbered and an X had been crossed through most of the squares.

Puzzling over it, he opened the notebook again and skimmed through its pages until he found a numbered list. Each item on the list had a date and a corresponding X. A few of the listings had notes beside them, such as 'check again' or 'minor hit, re-investigate'. Cross-referencing it to the map, he realized that the numbered list in the notebook corresponded to the numbered grid pattern on the property map.

"Holy shit," he whispered to the empty room around him. "It's a treasure map."

9

Sunday Mass - Droning priest - The Sundowner - A separate booth - Unfurling a map - Martyr of the family - Rekindled feud - Hungry kittens

SUNDAY MORNING AT Saint Margaret's Catholic church, an almost full house. Lee sat in the pew beside his parents and tried not to yawn at the droning monotone voice of Father Brody. He had stopped going to church years ago, which had caused no small consternation with his mother who had insisted that he was too young to make that kind of decision for his eternal soul. This Sunday service was different, however, as it would be partly in honor of his deceased grandmother and Lee was obliged to attend. He noted that most of his cousins had been browbeaten into attending also. Zoe sat across the aisle with Aunt Fran and poor Uncle Don. Two rows up sat Jeremy with Aunt Sally and Uncle Rob. Aunt Sally, the most pious of the clan, always sat up front and was the first to rise during the hymns. Back near the baptismal font, he had spotted Truman with Uncle Bill and Aunt Carol. Truman was smartly turned out in a smart salmon-colored shirt and thin tie. Even the cast on his arm looked somewhat fashionable like it was an accessory instead of a burden.

Seated in the row before Lee and his parents was poor Aunt Pauline, the tragic aunt who had stoically cared for Grandma Traven these last few years. Eldest of his father's siblings, Aunt Pauline was somewhat of a tragic figure among the clan. Married to Uncle Frank, the joker and teller of tall-tales, Pauline's only son had died in a boating accident when he was nineteen. Struck low by the loss, Pauline had only begun to recover when Uncle Frank up and vanished one night, abandoning her. There were rumors of another woman, of course, rumors that the loss of their son had unhinged him somehow, leading him to run off like a thief, but no one knew for sure.

Laid low by this second blow, Pauline had begun to crumble until Grandma Traven's condition worsened, requiring constant care. Pauline took up the task, saving herself through a sense of duty and purpose. But now that Grandma was gone, Aunt Pauline sat alone in the church pew and her siblings wondered what would become of her now.

At a cue from the droning priest, everyone dropped to the kneeler on the floor and then a moment later all were on their feet. Despite the monotony of the Mass, Lee noted the constant kneeling, standing, singing, and sitting must have been designed to prevent spiritual laggards such as himself from falling asleep. It worked.

After Mass, the priest stood on the church steps shaking hands with everyone as they left. Parishioners loitered in the parking lot, chatting and gossiping before climbing into their cars. There was a ritual to Sunday service that saw most parishioners retreat to the Sundowner Inn on the east side of town for their all-you-can-eat buffet and this Sunday was no different. Although the children of recently deceased Marion Rose Traven were still bickering, they all ended up at the Sundowner, standing in line with plates in hand, grumbling about the wait.

Having stuffed his gullet with scrambled eggs and too much bacon, Lee went to fetch more coffee from the urn. Scanning the long dining hall, he spotted Zoe sitting with her parents and waved her over to an empty booth.

She was wearing the same black dress she had worn to the funeral but accessorized with a long pendant chain and wedge heels. He had brought coffee for both of them and pushed her cup forward as she slid into the booth.

"You don't look too hungover," he said, eyeing her freshly scrubbed face and clear eyes. True hazel, but the flecks of green were only discernible up close.

"I didn't stay too long." She took two creamers from the tray on the table and emptied them into her cup. "Where did you disappear to last night?"

"I got bored, went home." Although the booth was apart from the other diners, he leaned in and lowered his voice. "Listen, there's something I want to show you."

Her left eyebrow arched up in a quizzical boomerang as he

reached into his jacket pocket. "Nothing disgusting, please. It's too early."

It was the map pilfered from the barn. Lee flattened it against the table top. "This," he said, "is a property map of the farm. See this grid drawn over it? Grandpa Traven mapped out the entire acreage for a ground search. Like they do with archaeological digs and stuff."

Leaning in for a closer look, Zoe traced an un-manicured finger over the penciled grid. "Quite the commitment. What are these numbers?"

"A way to track everything. He was dead serious about finding this thing. Each number on the grid was recorded in his notebook, marking the date it was searched and what he found, if anything. He was meticulously combing the entire property, square by square."

"And these X's crossed through each square? Does that mean they've been checked?"

"Yup."

Her finger ran along the map to the eastern edge of the grid system. There were two squares not marked with an X. "And these two? He skipped these last ones?"

Lee shook his head. "No, he didn't get that far. The last entry in the notebook was five years ago."

She shrugged, losing interest. "So?"

"Don't you get it?"

"Get what? That Grandpa had a weird hobby?"

"Grandpa died before he could finish the search." He tapped a finger against the two empty squares of the grid. "It could still be out there."

"What, the pirate treasure thing?" she said, letting out an abrupt laugh. "Lee, come on. This is crazy kid's stuff."

Forcing himself to be still, he took a breath and said: "But what if it's not? What if it's still out there?"

"And what if there really is a Santa Claus?" she countered. "Who cares?"

He tapped the two unchecked units on the map. "There's less than an acre left to search. Help me look for it."

"Why would I do that?"

"Because. It's buried treasure." His hand reached out and took hold of hers. "We'll split it."

She almost laughed, dismissing the idea but then her eyes fell to the unchecked squares on the map. A flutter of green lit up through the hazel. She was about to respond when another voice cut her off.

"What the hell is it with you two?"

Truman always had a knack for barging in at the wrong moment. His narrow eyes strafed the two of them before locking on the map spread across the table.

"What do you want?" Lee grunted.

"Push over," Truman said, almost body-checking Lee into the corner of the booth. "Always sneaking off, you two. What is that?"

Lee folded up the map. "Nothing."

"Let me see that," Truman said, pulling at the map.

Shoving his cousin aside, Lee got the map folded and tucked

inside his jacket. "Fuck off."

"You're a sneaky little shit, Lee."

Zoe shrugged, unamused at the two of them. "What's the big deal? Just show him."

Before Lee could respond, a cacophony of loud voices broke out over the already loud buffet room of the Sundowner. Lee looked up in shame to see his father on his feet, yelling at Aunt Pauline. More of them were rising, including Truman's and Jeremy's parents, to join in the fracas.

"That is such bullshit!" bellowed Lee's dad. "You loved them more so you deserve a bigger piece of the pie?"

Pauline's hands balled into knotty fists. "I was the one who stepped up when mom needed help. The rest of you couldn't be bothered!"

"Get off the cross already," Grant Traven yelled back. "I helped out."

Aunt Fran shook her fist. "You bought groceries in. Once!"

Lee sank down in the booth to hide as he listened to his father berate his siblings. Then it was Zoe and Truman's turn to hang their heads in mortification, unable to escape the shrill sounds of their own parents as they shouted down the room.

Jeremy was at the buffet table, helping himself to thirds. Lee watched his face turn red in shame at the public outburst.

"Jesus," Zoe sighed. "Now that is dead embarrassing."

"No shit," Truman agreed, keeping his head down as the voices got louder. Aunt Sally, exploding in tears, rushed from the room. "I'd hate to be their kids," he added.

———— ◆◆◆◆ ————

Among the Traven clan, there was only one who did not ever attend church, not even for drunken midnight Mass. Uncle Elvis often joked that he would burst into flames if ever set foot inside Saint Margaret's and half the family was inclined to believe him. To the more devout of the family, he would go out of his way to malign the character of dour old Father Brody, suggesting darkly that the man got up to no good with the altar boys in the confessional booth. How that angered Aunt Pauline and Aunt Sally.

While the Traven family feuded over the buffet brunch, Elvis drove out to the farm. Climbing out of his dented pickup truck, he looked up to regard the crows perched on the power lines above and smiled.

"It's your lucky day, you little bastards," he called out to the black rooks. "I left my shotgun at home."

Scanning the ground before him, he picked out a rock and tested its weight in his hand before taking aim and firing it at the birds. The crows alighted from the power line, flapped about for a moment before settling back onto the same length of line. They cawed at him as if taunting his aim.

"Bastards," he said, moving around the back of the truck. Lowering the tailgate, he hoisted up a large bag of dry feed onto his shoulder and sauntered toward the barn. Inside, he set the bag down and ripped open the top. Four clumsy kittens scampered toward him across the cobble floor and padded back and forth over his boots.

"Hold your horses," he said, scooping two bowls of kibble and setting them onto the floor. The small cats tucked in immediately and he folded up the end of the crinkly bag and set it high up on a shelf.

Brushing his hands, he glanced up to see the door to the workshop was open. Crossing into the inner room he flicked on the overhead bulb and frowned at the workbench. The drop cloth had been pulled away and the tools disturbed. Some of the books were gone, along with the large map that hung on the wall.

"Son of a bitch."

Turning to a plastic bin near the door he plucked out a length of chain and a padlock and marched back outside, stopping only to rub the head of the smallest kitten in the litter. Back out in the strong sunlight, the crows on the power lines began cawing at him again.

10

A rendezvous - Questions unsaid - Chains and a dead crow - Interlopers in an empty field - Kinsmen - A pact

"WHERE ARE YOU going?" his mother asked.

Still wolfing down his dinner, Lee brought his plate to the counter and marched for the door. "Out," he mumbled.

His father looked up from his meal and narrowed his eyes at his son. "Out where?"

"Just out. Don't wait up."

Rushing out to the garage, he stuffed a flashlight, compass, and gloves into his backpack. Scanning the shelves and bench for anything else he might need, he added a length of nylon rope, a can of orange spray paint and some wooden stakes. Slinging the pack over his shoulder he went out to the end of the driveway and waited. He checked the time on his phone, considered texting her again but held off. Looking up at the sun hovering over the western rim, he tried to guess how much daylight they'd have.

Not a lot. When he looked down, he saw the Volvo station wagon roll up.

Jumping into the passenger seat, he smiled at her. "I thought maybe you changed your mind."

Zoe pulled away from the curb and gunned the pedal. "This is a stupid idea."

"I know."

She steered the car out of town and down along Route 9 toward the family farm. Lee sat silently watching the houses thin out as they entered the rolling countryside.

"Thanks for doing this. I mean, I appreciate it."

Zoe relaxed into the seat, hanging one elbow out the window. "I'm still not sure why I agreed."

"Yes, you do," he said. "Because you got nothing better to do."

He turned on the radio and flicked through the dial. Country music or banal pop songs. He kept surfing.

"Just pick something," she said.

He left it on an oldies country station, just to annoy her. Marty Robbins sang about El Paso City. "So what's university like?"

"I love it," she said, her phantom dimple making a brief appearance. "My classes were tough but the profs were great. And I met so many awesome people. Not just awesome, but different, you know?"

Lee nodded as if he knew what she meant. "Different is good."

"You don't realize how small your world is until you meet people from other places," she said, warming to the subject. "The world you're from isn't the only way of life or even the right way of life. It's just one way among many."

"How so?" The question was asked in earnest but he hated how ignorant it sounded.

"Take my friend Jamie for example. She has two moms, both artists who traveled the world. They lived this sort of gypsy life, wandering from here to India and then to Vietnam. Total vagabonds, right? A year living on a houseboat in Amsterdam. And Jamie home-schooled the whole time."

"Home-schooled?" Lee asked, unable to contain his skepticism. "How'd that turn out?"

Zoe smirked at him. "Jaimie's one of the wisest people I've ever met. Not just smart, but wise. Do you know the difference?"

"Sure," he lied.

The station wagon slowed as she turned into the long driveway and the car bobbed along over the dips and potholes. Her eyes were fixed on the road as she steered around the worst of the rutted chasms and Lee chanced a glance at her. She had changed, grown. Moved on beyond this hick town. Even now, she was gone. She was beside him in the car but, in truth, she was back there at university.

"You got a boyfriend?"

"I met a couple guys," she replied with a shrug but didn't elaborate.

"No one special?"

"It was just kind of...meh. You know? I had enough on my hands keeping up with my classes and stuff. I made a vow first week of school that I wasn't going to get caught up in some dude."

She glanced at him with a proud smile. "And I stuck to it."

The old farmhouse flashed up in the headlights as she trundled the car past it and stopped before the graying mass of the barn.

"What about you?" she asked, turning the car off. "You seeing anybody?"

"Who am I gonna see?"

"Uh, hello?" she mocked. "Girls at school?"

He let off a chuckle. "Have you seen the girls at school?"

"Hey. Some of those girls are my friends."

"What, your fan club?"

With the engine silenced, the sound of crickets swarmed in through the open windows. He reached for the door handle but stopped and looked at her. "Things really sucked after you left."

She plucked the keys from the ignition. "I'm sure they weren't that bad."

He turned to look at her but she kept her eyes straight ahead on the barn before them. Not knowing what else to do, he laid his cards on the table. "You're like, the only friend I got, Zee. But you split."

She bristled at that. "That's not fair."

"I know. It's just..." His voice trailed off, leaving words unstated.

"Wait a minute," she said, holding up one hand. "Is that what this is about? Because if it is, I'm turning around right now."

"It isn't." He flung open the door and launched out of the car. "Come on."

Zoe followed, coming up behind him.

"Shit," he said.

"What is it?"

"This," he grunted. A chain was looped through the handles of the barn doors, secured with a padlock.

"So much for that idea."

"Shit," Lee said again.

Something dark and wet lay pushed up against the foot of the bay door. Zoe took a step closer, squinting against the shadows. "What is that?"

He nudged it with his sneaker. Black feathers and a beak the color of charcoal. Its head flopped to one side, loose and boneless.

"Gross!"

Zoe took a step back from the dead crow. "Why is it there?"

"I don't know."

"Did someone put it there? Maybe we should leave."

Turning away from the dead bird, Lee moved along the side of the barn until he came to a small window. Digging into his backpack, he produced the screwdriver and jacked the blade into the window seam.

"Uhm…" she sounded, scanning around them as if worried they would be caught. "Should you be doing that?"

The window creaked under the strain and then popped out of its frame. Lee pushed it open. "Help me up," he said.

With a boost from Zoe's cupped hands, he clambered over and dropped to the floor. A moment later the side-door unlatched and swung back. Lee waved her inside.

"Did you get hurt?" she asked, noting a slight limp.

"I'm fine," he said, flinging back the canvas from the workbench. He handed her the metal detector and then took a spade, a can of construction orange spray paint and a kerosene lantern.

She thumbed the device on, listening to the initial whine of the sensor. "What now?"

"We find the spot where Grandpa left off, then we sweep the ground with the metal detector until we find the lost treasure of Jesse James."

Beaming stupidly, he hurried from the barn. She exhaled loudly. It still seemed daft but she followed him out into the field anyway.

Following a tractor path of rutted grooves, they marched into the field and took their bearings. An open plain of rolling fields on one side, a stand of trees on the other, a hill in the distance. In the middle of a field of untended barley stood a single great oak tree like an island in the sea.

Zoe surveyed the landscape. "Where do we start?"

Lee dropped to one knee and unfurled the map on the ground. He pointed to a few distinct landmarks among the grid pattern. "We hike south across this field toward the creek." Looking up again, he pointed at a spot in the distance. "That way. I think."

"South is that way," she said, indicating a different course.

"Are you sure?"

She reached into the backpack on his shoulders and dug out the compass, holding it still in her hand. Smirking, she nodded at her plotted course. "South."

Gathering up the map they started advanced into the knee-high weeds. Zoe held the compass before her, course-correcting as they went. When she stopped suddenly, he stopped also and looked at her.

"What is it?"

"Do you hear that?"

A low rumbling drone, growing louder by the minute. A vehicle approaching, by the sound of it but as they swept the horizon nothing appeared.

"Shit," Lee spat. "We should hide."

Zoe looked around. They were stranded in the middle of the barley field. "Where?"

The rumbling noise flared louder and suddenly they could see it. An all-terrain-vehicle bounding across the plain with two riders, their faces hidden under helmets.

Lee's face soured. "Fuck's sakes. What are they doing here?"

"Who is it?" Zoe asked, shielding her eyes from the low-angled sun.

"Your cousins."

The ATV roared up before them and shut down. The helmets were plucked off to reveal Jeremy with Truman as the passenger.

"I knew you two were up to something," Truman said, grinning as he set the helmet on the seat.

Lee tried to sound casual but, given the circumstances, that was impossible. "What do you want?"

"What do you got?"

"Dead crows and a pile of shit. Help yourself."

Jeremy came about and took the metal detector from Zoe. "What the hell are you two after?"

Lee reached for the Buccaneer 2000. "Gimme that."

Jeremy, the tallest among them by a head, held the device high, taunting his younger cousin. "Jump for it, ya little shit."

"Knock it off, Jeremy," Zoe said. She held out her hand and the hockey player relinquished the detector to her.

Truman eyed the odd-looking device in her hands before turning to Lee. "So what's the big secret? Did Grandpa bury a jar quarters out here?"

"Get lost, Truman. No one asked you to come."

Truman just grinned at him. "Zoe says you're hunting for money. What money?"

Lee shot her a dirty look, to which she shrugged in response. He kept silent.

"What money?"

"Jesse James' money."

Jeremy's laughter was loud and abrupt. "No shit? Hell, just last week I found Dracula's skateboard buried in my backyard!"

No one else laughed, especially Truman. Dead sober, he said: "We want in."

"Get bent," Lee replied. "This is ours."

"Ah, but it's not just yours, is it?" Truman swept his cast-clad arm across the lonely plain surrounding them. "If it's on Grandpa's farm, then it belongs to all of us."

Lee regarded the two young men and then met Zoe's gaze. All she offered was a bemused shrug. Behind her, a murder of crows alighted to the stranded oak tree and cawed to them.

"It would be faster," she suggested, "with four instead of two."

Jeremy was still chuckling over the whole idea, surprised that everyone was taking the idea seriously. "Come on," he scolded Truman. "You really believe this shit?"

Truman regarded his three cousins, squaring each one in the eye as he proposed a pact. "Whatever we find, we split four ways."

Lee didn't budge, maintaining a flinty silence. The crows in the tree carried on their mindless trilling.

"Dude," Truman said patiently, "we're family."

"This is my gig," Lee stated. "My idea. We do it my way."

"Done."

Even Jeremy felt the tension ease. "Ahh," he mocked, approaching his cousins with open arms. "Let's hug it out."

Lee pressed the shovel into his hands. "Make yourself useful."

11

Folktales - Uncle Frank and Aunt Pauline - A crocodile in the creek - Lost - The stone fence - Running the twine - Sweeping the ground - False target

THE BRIGHT ORB of the sun hovered over the treeline to the west as the quartet trudged through the neglected barley. At a distance, with their spades and lantern and metal-witching device, they might have seemed like a band of dwarfs off to the mythical ore mines.

Lee held fast to the Buccaneer detector, eager to field-test it. Despite the intrusion of the two newcomers, he tingled with a frisson of glee at the prospect ahead. Twenty paces on he found himself marching lockstep beside Truman.

"Do you know the story?"

Truman offered a half-shrug, striding through the weeds on his long legs. "I remember hearing kooky stories when I was a kid about Jesse James and stuff. How he was family and hid out here when he was running from the law."

Lee plucked the head off a strand of barley and let it crumble through his fingers. "Who used to tell those stories? Was it Uncle Rob?"

"I think it was Uncle Frank. He was always telling us crazy stories. Remember that time he had us convinced there was an alligator in the creek?"

Lee smiled at the memory. "None of us went near the creek that whole summer. He even had me convinced I'd seen it."

"It's too bad the nutcase took off," Truman said. "I used to like his bullshitting."

Alongside being a spinner of tall tales, Uncle Frank had been an oddly eccentric relation, often rivaling crazy Uncle Elvis in the weirdo relation category. Five years prior, Uncle Frank had packed a bag and slipped off into the night, never to be seen again.

Lee scratched his head at the memory. "Why did Uncle Frank take off? Did he owe someone money?"

"Who knows? Maybe Aunt Pauline finally pushed him over the edge with her hypochondria."

Poor Aunt Pauline had never been the same since the night her husband disappeared. She had become sullen and bitter in the interim, her self-diagnosis of varying illnesses ushering her down a path of acute self-medication.

"Frank used to love that Jesse James story," Truman remarked. "I always figured it was bullshit, like the rest of his tall tales."

"Grandpa believed it. I asked my old man about it. He said Grandpa was obsessed with finding it."

"Everyone needs a hobby," Truman said.

They went ten more paces before Lee stopped and scanned the field around him. Dropping the backpack, he consulted the map again.

"What's wrong?" Zoe asked, coming alongside.

Lee nodded to a grove of cottonwood trees further on. "There's supposed to be an old stone fence here."

Jeremy groaned. "Great. We're lost."

Zoe looked up at the sky where the sun was hitting the trees. "We're still moving south, aren't we?"

"I thought we were." Lee dug for the compass and held it up, watching the needle spin and spin. "What's wrong with this thing?"

Zoe took it from him and waited for the needle to settle on its cardinal point but it continued to arc lazily around its fluid-filled shell. "Either it's broken or there's something out here messing up the magnetic field."

"Nice work, retard," added Jeremy.

"Probably an alien crash site," Truman suggested. He slipped his phone from his back pocket and tapped the screen.

"What are you doing?"

"Water-witching." He held the phone out before him, following the flashing indicator on the screen. "I'm just taking a bearing with the GPS." After a moment, the phone chirped.

"This way."

The fence was old, fashioned out of stones plucked from the field by settlers who had cleared the field for crops two centuries ago. Three feet tall and crumbling in spots, the stone wall ran parallel to the creek bank like some medieval fortification. The treasure hunters approached its stone face and dropped their gear to the weeds.

"This is it," announced Lee, needlessly.

"All right," said Truman. "What now?"

Lee studied the stone wall before them. "There should be a marker of some kind that Grandpa used for his grid."

"What does it look like?" Zoe asked.

"I don't know. Could be a stake in the ground or spray paint on something. Anything."

"That's helpful," Jeremy complained.

The four of them spread out, searching the stone wall and the weed-choked ground for a sign. Minutes ticked by before Truman called out, bringing the others running.

"Is this it?" he asked, pointing to a patch of neon orange paint on the stone wall.

"It's gotta be." Lee knelt down for a closer look. Patchy and eroded by the elements, the painted slash marks appeared to be a number. "Does that look like 112?"

"Hard to tell," Truman answered. "116?"

Digging out the map again, Lee tried to orient their spot between the wall, the creek beyond it and the open plain behind them. He nodded to the eastern run of the stone fence. "See if there's another mark on the wall that way."

Zoe was already moving along the perimeter, scanning the

stones as she went. "How far down?"

"I dunno. Ten yards? Maybe twenty?"

Moments later she called out, holding up something overhead, and the others dashed forward to see a wooden stake in her hand, the top of which had been sprayed with the same neon orange.

"There's another number on the wall, too," she said, pointing the stake at an orange slash on the stones. "That is clearly 117."

Lee dropped to one knee. He pressed a fingertip to the mark. Paint flaked away. "This is it."

Jeremy looked on, unimpressed. "What are the numbers for?"

"Each square on the grid is numbered. Grandpa crossed out each square he searched." Lee laid the map down and pointed at the two squares of unmarked grid space. "The last grid searched was 117."

Truman compared the map against the length of wall before them. "So this way, starting from the creek and then north."

"All the way up to that stand of poplars," Lee confirmed.

Jeremy sunk the spade into the ground and rested an elbow on the handle. "So what now?"

"We use the stakes and the twine to map out our own grid," Lee replied. "Then we sweep the ground with the metal detector."

"Until it beeps," Zoe added.

Jeremy eye-balled the distance between copse of poplar trees in the distance and their position near the wall. "That's gonna take all night."

"Then go home," Lee said. "No one asked you here."

They got to work hammering in the first stake in the ground

and running the spool of twine out into the field. Truman used his phone's GPS to pinpoint where the next stake was to be planted. When they were done they had a run of land marked out from the creek all the way to the treeline.

"We'll work in shifts," Lee said, scrounging the can of spray paint from his backpack and shook it. "I'm gonna start at the far end and work my way back. I'll mark my spot with paint and then someone else can take over."

"Let me see the map," Truman said.

"The map stays with me."

"Don't be so freaking paranoid."

Lee hesitated but felt his other two cousins staring at him. He handed the map to Truman and gathered up the metal detector, fitting the headphones over his ears. The Buccaneer beeped on start-up then fell silent.

"Get cracking, Dr. Jones," Truman said. "Find us a treasure."

They watched Lee march into the swaying barley. Three crows flapped up and took flight at his approach, wheeling through the air above him.

Jeremy maintained his foul mood. "Now what?"

"We wait our turn," Zoe said.

"Anybody bring snacks?"

"I did," Truman replied. Hopping onto the uneven surface of the stone wall, he unzipped his backpack and pulled out a can of beer. He tossed the backpack to Zoe. "I brought enough for the whole class."

The coil end of the Buccaneer was a round disk that pulsed a signal into the earth and pinged when the return struck metal. Lee swept it over the ground, watching for any signal on the display panel. The panel was digital with a set of buttons and dials underneath, none of which made sense to him. The readout signaled in percentages, which he assumed measured the amount of metal present in the ground or the density of it. He scolded himself for not figuring out how the Buccaneer operated earlier but he assumed that Grandpa must have set the device to ping for what he was seeking. From there it was simply a matter of waving the coil over the ground until it beeped.

He worked the span of the staked area in a meter-long sweep, moving crossways from one run of the twine to the other before moving down one yard to start over. The digital numbers on the display ticked up and down by a few digits as he went, but there was no tell-tale beep from the device. Judging the distance from his position to where his cousins loitered down near the stone fence, he picked up the pace to cover each pass quickly. With dusk already on them, they didn't have much time left before night fell completely.

Ping.

The digital display suddenly spiked to 82 percent, accompanied by a piercing whine in the headphones. Lee froze and circled the coil over the area to pinpoint the target. He set the device down carefully, got out his trowel and stabbed at the parched earth. Dry salty dirt flew up but his blade didn't clunk down on anything solid like he had anticipated. Passing the detector over the hole, it pinged even louder, indicating that the target was still down there.

Clunk. The metal trowel bit against something with a clear, solid tang. Scooping out the dirt exposed the tip of a metal bar and his heart pounded harder. Wrenching it free, he brushed off the soil to reveal a simple iron spike. Old and interesting maybe, but otherwise worthless. It probably fell off some ancient harrower or harvester a century ago. Did he expect to get lucky right off the bat?

He backfilled the hole with the loose dirt and then stuck the spike in vertically to create a marker of sorts. Then he gathered up the Buccaneer and resumed his ground search.

Only an acre and a half left to go, he sighed to himself.

12

Jagging the nerves - Who doesn't love the dark? - The tedium of the treasure seeker - Throwing in the towel - Blue sky thinking - Heads or tails - Paydirt

THE CROWS QUIETED as the empty plain darkened before them and the hypnotic trill of crickets rose up around the small band of fortune hunters. With the daylight gone, the temperature dropped to the point where a low mist was rising like smoke from the rippling creek.

"This is fucking stupid," Jeremy announced.

Truman sat studying the map in the glow of lantern light and ignored his cousin's belly-aching. Although as strong as a draft horse and almost as tall, Truman knew his cousin to be of a frail nature. Pampered was a term he'd used more than once to silence the hockey player's griping habit.

"You're free to leave or to stay, Jay," he said. "But you've hit your limit in the complaints department for one night."

"I'm just saying, man. It's stupid."

Truman tore his eyes from the map to regard his cousin. "And now you've repeated it for the fourth time. So pick a different topic of conversation or shut the hell up. Okay?"

Observing one then the other, Zoe said: "We could talk about how creepy it is out here. Now that it's dark."

"Scared?" Jeremy asked.

"No. I love the dark."

"But you're shivering," Truman stated.

She tucked her knees up and wrapped her arms around her shins, realizing she hadn't dressed properly for the excursion. Then again, what exactly does one wear to a half-assed treasure hunt? "I'm just cold. The temperature dropped really fast."

"We should make a campfire," Jeremy suggested hopefully. Anything to distract from the boredom would be a boon at this point.

Truman nixed the idea. "No fire. Someone might see it."

"Killjoy."

The churn of the crickets continued, rising in volume. Something scuttled through the darkness on their left, startling them all.

"Was that a gopher?" Zoe asked, peering into the dark. Whatever it was, it was gone now.

"Maybe it was the creek crocodile," Jeremy suggested.

Her eyes lit up. "I'd almost forgotten that story. Didn't Uncle Frank have a name for it? Cranky the crocodile or something?"

"Crotch-rot?"

"No, that wasn't it. Truman, do you remember?"

No answer. Truman's eyes were fixed on the unspooled map.

"Hello? Earth to Truman."

"I think this map is wrong," Truman said.

Zoe moved closer to the ring of light cast by the lantern. "Wrong how?"

"The fence here," he said, pointing at the low wall of fieldstone. "That marks the border of the farmland, right. But on the map, the property line extends past it, right down to the creek itself."

"So what?" Jeremy butt in.

"It's just weird. See here? It even goes past the creek to include the bank on the other side."

"That is odd," Zoe said, hunkering down to see the map. "The creek would be a natural border. What's the date on this map?"

Truman shrugged. "Ninety-three."

"Boundaries change over time." She ran her finger over the blurred typeset in the margins of the map. "The property line may have moved since this map was published."

Truman cocked an eyebrow, affronted at her knowledge on something that he was ignorant of. "Why do you know so much about maps?"

"I like maps," she said as if surprised at the question. "My dad showed me how to read them."

Something dropped into the band of lantern light, tipping onto the edge of the map. The long handled metal detector. Zoe and Truman straightened up to see Lee flop into the grass before them, dejection written across his features.

"Anything?" Zoe asked, faking cheerfulness.

"Nothing. Pieces of junk." He noted the cans of beer in each of their hands. "What the hell? You guys having a party without me?"

Truman tugged a beer from his backpack and thrust it at him. "Relax, cuz."

Popping the tab, Lee took a long slug and then looked at his compadres. "Who's next?"

"Next?" Jeremy sneered. "It's too dark to carry on. Let's split."

"I'll do it," Truman said. "Where'd you leave off?"

Lee pointed back at the way he came. "Fifty paces in. I marked the spot with the spray paint."

"Semper fucking fi." Snatching up the Buccaneer 2000, Truman rushed into the darkness, bouncing the beam of a flashlight before him.

Lee wiped the foam from his lips. "What time is it?"

"Almost eleven," she said.

Jeremy shook his head. With Truman gone, he expelled the complaints bubbling up inside his breast. "This is a freakin' waste of time."

Lee regarded his cousin with open contempt. "If it's such a waste of time, why are you here?"

"Same as you," Jeremy shrugged. "I got fuck all else to do."

Zoe got to her feet and stretched, wishing she had brought a jacket. The evening chill had deepened, intensifying the mist ghosting over the field. Hearing a tinkling of metal, she looked down to see Lee empty his pockets onto the flat map.

"What is that stuff?"

He held up a rusted length of metal. "Just stuff I found. Most of it's junk. Except for this."

She took the large coin from his hand and rubbed the grit from its face. "It's just an old penny."

"Look at the date," he said.

Wetting her thumb, she scrubbed the dirt away to reveal the profile of a man in a feather headdress and the stamped date of 1878. "It's really old," she said with surprise. "Do you think it's worth anything?"

"Maybe. But more importantly, it fits the timeline."

"The Jesse James story?" She turned the coin to catch the light and examined the face again. "When did he die?"

"Eighteen-eighty something."

Jeremy moved closer, curiosity piqued at Lee's find. "Let me see."

Zoe looked out across the field, following the run of twine where it was swallowed by fog and darkness. "What do you think we'll find? I mean, assuming we find anything?"

Scrubbing the soil from a curved length of metal, Lee shrugged. "Dunno. Silver dollars. Maybe half-eagles or even double eagles."

"What's a half-eagle?" Jeremy asked.

"Coins from that era, made of solid gold. The face value of a half-eagle was five dollars, the double eagle was twenty. God knows what they're worth now."

Jeremy's neck craned forward, ears cocked. "Gold? Shit. We'd be rich."

"If the story's true," Zoe cautioned. "That's a big if'."

"Still, imagine it. It'd be like winning the lottery." The light from the lantern flashed hot in Jeremy's eyes. He looked at his cousins. "What are you gonna do if we strike it rich?"

Zoe laughed at the idea, while Lee shrugged and went back to studying the collected artifacts.

"Knock it off," Jeremy scoffed. "Don't pretend you haven't thought about it."

Lee looked up from his trove of rusted junk. "What are you gonna do?"

The light renewed in Jeremy's eyes, picturing something far off. "There's a training camp in Minnesota. The best one around but it's pricey."

"You'd still play hockey?" Zoe asked.

"Of course," he spoke reflexively. "It's all I've ever wanted."

Lee shook the penny in his hand and turned to her. "What about you?"

"Go back to university."

"Gimme a break," Jeremy muttered. "Who goes to school when they're rich?"

"I love school." She kept her eyes on the open field, expecting something to emerge from the thickening fog. "If I had my way, I'd be a career student."

Lee studied her face, shaded as it was in the weak light of their lantern. He almost startled when she turned abruptly, meeting his stare.

"What are you going to do?"

"I'm getting the hell out of here."

"Where are you going to go?"

Lee brushed the grit from his hands. "Doesn't matter. As long as it ain't here."

Truman returned from his expedition bearing the same forlorn expression that Lee had carried. Empty-handed, he let the Buccaneer fall to the grass. Zoe went next, eager to try her hand at metal-detecting. Jeremy lay sprawled on the hard earth, using one of the backpacks for a pillow.

Truman dug idly at the itchy skin under his cast. He nodded at the backpack next to Lee. "Is there any beer left?"

Lee reached into the bag and pulled out a single can. "Last one. Want to split it?"

"I'll flip you for it." He reached down for the tarnished copper on the map. "We'll use your fancy penny."

"Don't lose it," Lee said.

"Call it."

"Heads."

The copper bounced onto the paper map with a loud pop.

Truman thrust his cast into the air. "Tails! You lose!"

"No dice," Lee countered. "You gotta catch it. Go again."

"Screw you I have to catch it. It landed tits up, I win." He cracked open the beer and took a long, satisfied draw on it.

"You're such a cheater."

"Shut up for a second," Jeremy interjected. Bolting up, he motioned for them to be still. "Is that Zoe?"

The noise coming out of the fog was her voice, calling out loud and excited. All three of them scrambled to their feet.

"You got to be kidding me," Truman spat. "Ten minutes in and she finds something?"

"Grab a shovel," Lee said, snatching up the lantern and bolting away into the fog.

Twenty yards down the marked run they found Zoe waving the coil of the metal detector over a patch of dry earth. The squelching whine of the device cut through the gentle lulling of the crickets.

"What is it?"

"I don't know but it's big," Zoe answered. "Watch this."

The three males kept quiet as they watched her wave the coil over a wide swath of dirt. The high-pitched return signal indicated a large target underground.

Lee snatched the spade from Truman's hand and attacked the target, stabbing the earth and flinging the dirt away like a man possessed. The ground was hard, parched as it was from a lack of rain, and the digging was slow.

"Hold up," said Jeremy. "We gotta break it up first." Wielding the old pick-ax in hand, he swung it high and brought it down hard, piercing the soil with the point. It broke apart as he pried up chunks of earth and swung again. Within minutes the patch was broken up and Lee scooped the rubble away quickly. Waving his cousin back, Jeremy swung again at the ground but this time a metallic peel rang out and his hands stung from the vibration.

"I hit it."

"Dig for fuck's sakes!" cried Truman as he dropped to his knees and scooped out the dirt with his bare hands, using his cast like a plow.

They all dug, clawing at the soil until something solid graced their fingertips. They troweled away the dirt to find the edge of a round mass of metal encrusted with rust. Jeremy sprang up, fetching the pick-ax again.

"Back up," he growled, fitting the sharp end against the metal object and hauling back with everything he had. Thick cords bulged in his neck before the mass popped from its grave. The other three reached down and strained to haul it up onto the weeds. A round bowl with a hole in the bottom, damp earth clotted over the corroded rim.

Eyes wide and breathing hard, Zoe spoke first. "What is it?"

"A brake drum," Lee answered, lowering his head in dismay.

Jeremy let the heavy tool fall to the ground and stepped away. He turned his head to one side, spat into the weeds. "This is bullshit."

Truman scraped the dirt from the metal drum with his thumb. "Farm junk. There's bound to be a lot more of it out here."

"Screw this," Jeremy stated and walked away. "I'm going home."

"Jeremy..."

He stopped to level a scornful eye on Truman. "You want a ride home, get moving. If not, then stay here with these losers."

The remaining trio sat quietly regarding their corroded prize as the last of the adrenaline fizzled away.

Zoe was the first to stand. She set her sneaker against the brake drum and rolled it back into the hole. "Let's go home," she said and turned to follow Jeremy.

Truman shot up and offered his good hand to his cousin. Grasping it, Lee jerked to his feet but avoided his cousin's eyes and the two of them trailed after the others without another word between them.

13

Blackbirds - 12 Gauge - The broken window - A quiet rink - Outlaw history - Stranger in an expensive suit - Grandpa's death - The land developer - Ticking clock

THE CROW HOPPED about the rancid ear of corn on the ground, cocking its head this and that before it began to jab at its meal. When another blackbird approached, it cawed angrily to chase it off and bent again to the corn. Thus occupied, it failed to register the faraway click of a hammer being pulled back.

It exploded in a thunderous mess, the indigo feathers billowing into the air as the blast of the shotgun echoed through the fields, sending its brethren flapping away for safety. A second shot ripped the silence of the open sky, dropping another bird.

Fifty yards across the field of untended corn stalks, Uncle Elvis thumbed the lever and broke the shotgun at the hinge. Plucking out the spent casings, he blew the smoke from the fired bores of the twin barrels to cool the metal and eyed the remainder of crows flapping overhead. The blown shells were slipped into a pocket rather than discarded on the ground and then he slid fresh rounds into the bores and softly clicked the shotgun whole. Seating the gun stock against his shoulder, Elvis waited for the birds to settle again and then slowly brought the barrel up.

Two more thunderclaps ripped across the blue sky, echoing down the plain.

Striding in from the field, Elvis opened the driver's side door of his pickup and slipped the shotgun into its case before sliding the weapon into the cramped space behind the seat. Digging for the key to the Yale padlock, he turned toward the old barn only to stop cold in his tracks.

The small window in the side of the barn hung at a wrong angle, one square of glass missing from its pane. Crossing to it, he tilted the window open to find it jostled loosely from a wrenched hinge.

"Goddamn it," he uttered and eased the window down.

———◆◆◆———

The rink was quiet save for the slash of the teenage skating instructor and two little girls. Lee sat behind the concession stand with one of the pilfered Jesse James books open before him and a paper cup of coffee in his hand. He stopped occasionally to scribble the odd observation into a cheap notebook. The disappointment of the previous night's excursion had left him irritable but he wasn't willing to give up just yet. His grandfather was not crazy, despite what his own father claimed, and Lee thought that he could find evidence of it if he just looked harder. Going to the farm during the day was out of the question, so he turned to studying the available resources. Maybe there was something in all of these books about the famous outlaw that could help them.

After sketching out a basic timeline of Jesse James' life, he began making a list of all the places the bank robber was known to have lived. He had hoped to find evidence that James had traveled this far but the most northern location he could find was Northfield, Minnesota. He tried to uncover something that might link the James clan to the Traven family tree, but there was scant information on them. The James clan were believed to be of Irish stock, like that of the Travens but that connection was weak.

There were simply too many unknowns to try and string together any connective tissue between the outlaw and his own family line. What was it that made Grandpa so sure that the legend was real? Was it just blind faith? Or greed, plain and simple? What did he even know of Grandpa Traven? Little beyond a stooped old man and the smell of his cigars.

The sound of voices pulled him back to earth. Glancing behind him, he saw his father emerge from the office with another man, a stranger decked out in a nice suit and a white Stetson. A flashy watch that smelled of money. Or a smoke screen meant to convey success. He watched his father shake hands and share a last joke with the stranger.

On his way to the exit, the well-dressed man tipped his fancy cowboy hat at Lee. "How're the concession sales, son?" he said cheerfully.

Lee glanced over the empty arena. "Lousy."

"Time to hustle," he exclaimed as he pushed through the doors. "That popcorn won't sell itself."

The man vanished and Lee frowned. As usual, he thought of a good comeback thirty seconds after the fact. "Take a bag, pal, and choke on it."

Closing his book, he stepped out of the concession stand and made for the office. His father sat at his cramped desk, bent over a handful of papers.

"The pop machine is busted again," Lee announced.

His father turned a page in the paperwork but didn't bother to look up, said: "Call the service guy."

Lee leaned against the door frame and waited for his father to see him. It took a minute and when his father spoke, it was with annoyance.

"Anything else broken?"

Lee scratched his chin. "When did Grandpa die?"

"What?"

"Five years ago? Or six?"

"Five," his father replied. "May 23rd of that year, to be exact. Ruined everyone's long weekend, which was typical of the old man." His father removed his glasses to clean the lenses. "About the same time Uncle Frank took off, abandoning your Aunt Pauline."

"How did he die?"

His father stiffened at the query. "Who said Uncle Frank died? He packed a bag and vanished."

"No, Grandpa. How did he die?"

Grant Traven rubbed at the stubble on his chin, unsure whether to answer his son. "Don't you have work to do?"

"There's just Tracey and her students here," Lee answered. "So? How did Grandpa die?"

"A hunting accident."

Lee furrowed his brow. "I thought he had a heart attack?"

"He was shooting crows in the back forty, shot himself in the foot. That's what brought on the heart attack."

Lee tilted his head back in surprise. "Shot his foot? No one ever told me that."

"Not something you tell a 12-year-old kid." Rising from the desk, Grant gathered up a small bundle of envelopes and pressed them into his son's hands, "Drop these in the mail. And stop by Rodrigo's to see when he can come look at the Zamboni."

Lee fanned through the stack of envelopes. "Who was that slick guy you were talking to?"

"Big Bill Daggett. Land developer."

A chill slithered down Lee's spine. "What does he want?"

"The farm." Lee's father looked up at his son, surprised to see him still loitering. "What's with all the questions?"

Lee almost stuttered. "You're really gonna sell the farm?"

"That's the plan. The acreage is huge and Big Bill is looking for the right place to build his next subdivision. The farm is exactly what they're looking for, what with the creek nearby and the wooded lot. And they'll pay mightily for it." Grant Traven tilted back in his chair, his gaze streaming out far beyond the painted cinderblock walls of the office. "The real obstacle is getting your aunts and uncles to agree on selling the land instead of bickering over who's entitled to what. Jesus help me."

Lee leaned back, catching the bad news hard. "That's a bit quick, isn't it?"

"Not quick enough. Bill's been eyeing that property since your grandfather died, seeing the potential of the place way back then. Now's the time to strike a deal, while he's still got a boner for it. End of the week is my goal. Papers signed, deal done."

Lee gritted his molars. "End of the week?"

"God willing. But it all depends on my dipshit siblings agreeing on the deal. I have my work cut out for me."

Silence crept across the floor as Lee scrambled for a counter-argument, one that didn't sound ridiculous. He knew that it would come to him five minutes too late.

His father made a dismissive wave of his hand, shooing his son back out to the rink area. "Go mail that stuff. And call the service guy about the pop machine."

<hr />

The enemy kept coming, surging forward in waves, some armed with automatic weapons, others with nothing more than a club in their hands and murder in their eyes. Jeremy strafed them with gunfire, mowing down wave after wave of attackers as they sprang up behind burned-out cars. One combatant's head exploded with gore as the .50 cal blew it apart, another was cut in half, but there was no end to the assault. For every enemy that went down under his fire, another two sprang up in its place and when Jeremy's rifle clicked empty, the attackers swarmed over him and the screen splattered red.

"Fuck!" he snarled, almost crushing the game controller in his hand. In his gaming career, he had destroyed a number of control pads; hurling them against the wall or simply crushing them in his powerful grip.

He had been playing Fallout for weeks and no matter how hard he tried, he could not advance past this stage. He began to suspect that there was no level after this, that the game was set to fail by making this stage impossible.

"This friggin' game is rigged, man."

The workbench that used to hold his father's tools now held a flat-screen TV and the gaming console. Little by little, Jeremy had taken over the garage, turning it into his own private space. His father's complaints about having nowhere to park his car were ignored as Jeremy slowly squeezed him out, adding a secondhand sofa and a fake Persian rug to cover the slab floor. In one corner was the drum kit that he never played anymore and in the opposite end was the bench press and weights that he used daily. The only vehicle in the garage was his ATV, parked just inside the roll-up doors. The mud flaps and undercarriage were crusted in mud and straw from his last outing across the untended fields of the Traven farm.

Jeremy tossed the game controller in the direction of his guest. "You want a turn?"

Truman didn't reply. Stretched out on a lawn chair with his feet up on the fender of the King Quad, he was absorbed in the book he was reading.

Annoyed, Jeremy grunted at him. "Yo. You're up."

"You go," Truman replied without looking up.

Lame, Jeremy concluded. Still, he was curious. "What's Harry Potter up to these days?"

Truman turned the page. There was a pencil tucked behind his ear. He removed it and underlined a passage but did not reply.

"What is that?" Jeremy asked. Truman angled the book for him to see the cover. *Jesse James: Last Rebel of the Civil War.* The book was thick, the pages dense with small typeset and footnotes. He turned his nose up in disgust. "Are you kidding me?"

Truman underlined another sentence. "It's a good book."

"You're falling for this shit, too? Dude, give it up."

Setting the book onto his lap, Truman raised his eyes to his meet his cousin's. "Did you know that this guy manipulated his own public image? He'd write letters to the newspapers, claiming his innocence. All while robbing banks and trains. He's like a politician or a movie star, controlling his own press."

"Who cares?" Jeremy said, rolling his eyes.

"I do. I want to know who this guy was. And not just the comic book legend." Truman opened the book again, finding his place. Pencil at the ready, to crib notes in the margins. "Turns out gold fever ran in this dude's family. When Jesse's a little kid, his old man, a preacher no less, hears about the gold rush out in California. He drops everything and heads west, abandoning his family."

Jeremy raised his head, despite himself. "No shit. Did he strike it rich?"

"No. He loses everything and dies of cholera or something. Penniless." Eyes brightened, he laughed like it was a punchline.

"Karma's a bitch." Jeremy laid back on the bench press and gripped the bar suspended above him. Then he paused. "What happened to Jesse? Did he ride off into the sunset with a ton of money?"

"No," Truman replied, chortling with an odd laugh. "But get this, he gets shot in the back by one of his own men."

Jeremy lowered the bar to his chest and pushed up it up, listening to his cousin laugh. Truman's sense of humor was strange, to say the least, and Jeremy had stopped trying to understand it a long time ago.

14

The Wayfarer - Measured out in coffee spoons - The quartet reunited - A house divided - Vicious boys - A visit from the King - Pale son

THE WAYFARER DINER, situated at the corner of Main and Elm, had changed little since the day it opened in 1962. A long lunch counter with spinning stools, wide booths that accommodated five patrons and a hotel bell that clanged when an order was ready to be taken to a table. The only thing that seemed to change was the patrons themselves, plodding on from teenagehood to middle-age to doddering seniority, stirring their coffee cups while complaining about the weather.

The bell rang again and the waitress brought a heaping platter of bacon and eggs to the farthest booth. Jeremy tucked into it immediately. Across the table, Truman stirred spoon after spoon of sugar into his coffee cup.

Jeremy paused his late breakfast, watching his cousin. "Dude, what the hell? Why don't you just mainline the whole thing."

"I need a pick-me-up," Truman said, stirring the sludge at the bottom of his cup. "But this will have to do."

"That shit will kill you."

Truman looked down in disgust at the mess of runny egg whites and greasy bacon his companion was shoveling down his gullet. "You're worse than a fucking girl, you know that? Healthy this and body-conscious that. Don't you get tired of the protein shakes and calorie counting?"

"I don't want junk in my system. Simple as that."

Setting his cup down, Truman's cast clunked against the table. He was formulating a clever way to skewer his cousin's vain body obsession when Zoe appeared before them, sinking his train of thought.

"I just got Lee's message," she said, sliding onto the seat next to Jeremy. "What's the emergency?"

"Search me," Jeremy said. "The douchebag hasn't shown up yet."

Zoe pilfered a strip of bacon from his plate. "Don't be nasty."

The hockey player almost pouted at his diminished meal. "The little shit had us up all night chasing fairy tales."

"Did he twist your arm?" she challenged.

Truman went on stirring his coffee, clanking the spoon against the cup as he observed the other two. He looked at Zoe. "Why do you always defend him?"

"Why do you guys always pick on him?"

"See," Truman said, "You're doing it again. Do you feel sorry for him or something? Charity work for the socially retarded?"

"Who's retarded?" said a new voice.

The trio's eyes rose to find the topic of discussion join the table. Jeremy laughed, spitting crumbs as Lee pushed in. Truman slid over to make room, smiling at the newcomer.

"Your timing is impeccable, cuz."

"Ignore them," Zoe said impatiently. "What's the emergency?"

Lee took a breath. He had raced over here on his bike as soon as he could slip away from the arena. "The parental units are selling the farm to some land developer. The deal could close within days."

Jeremy let his fork drop noisily against the plate. "That's your big emergency? Get the hell outta here."

Truman perked up. "Where'd you hear this?"

"My old man. He's setting up the deal. All he has to do is get everyone to agree to sell."

Zoe stole a wedge of dry toast from Jeremy's plate. "Well, that's not gonna happen soon. Not the way they're fighting."

"I wouldn't be so sure about that," countered Truman. "Property that size is gonna fetch big money. And I mean big. They'll change their minds as soon as they see the potential payday."

Jeremy slapped Zoe's sneaking hand away from his meal. "Good. The sooner they sell it, the sooner they'll all stop fighting. I've never seen my mom so angry."

"You're missing the point," Lee stated. "The developer wants to rush this through and close the deal now. That doesn't leave us much time to find this thing before they close off the whole area."

Jeremy wiped his mouth, crumpled up the napkin and tossed it contemptuously at his cousin. "Who gives a shit? I ain't going back."

Lee pushed the napkin aside. "Why not?"

"It's a waste of time."

"Don't you want to find it?"

Jeremy shook his head. "It's a fairy tale, you idiot. There is no treasure."

"What if you're wrong? What if it's out there and this land developer guy finds it when they bulldoze the site?" It was Lee's turn to shake his head. He turned to Zoe, pleading his case. "Tell him, Zoe."

Buttering the last triangle of toast, she tried to soften the blow. "I think Jeremy's right. It's just an old folktale. We should leave it alone."

Lee leaned back in shock. Even Truman was caught out by her reply.

"I'm sorry," she said.

In the intervening silence, the waitress swept in with the steaming pot in hand. "More coffee?"

"No," Jeremy announced. "We're done here."

"I'll bring the bill."

The waitress moved on, leaving the quartet sitting in silence, arms folded in deadlock.

"Fine," Lee said. "I'll do it alone."

"Knock yourself out," Jeremy said. He nudged Zoe gently.

"Scooch out, Zee."

She got to her feet, allowing her cousin to launch himself out of the booth.

Truman began to grin as if he couldn't be more pleased with the day. Lifting his cup, he tilted it toward Lee in a toast. "Looks like it's just you and me, kid."

"Leave it alone," Zoe said again. "It's just trouble."

"You two can bugger off," Truman said, continuing to flash his grin. "Me and Scooby-Doo here will split the shares."

"You're both fucking crazy," Jeremy called back as he pushed out the door.

Zoe lingered, standing before the booth and Lee looked up at her with hangdog eyes, awaiting her verdict. She offered a shrug. "I have to go."

Lee watched as she strode away, following Jeremy out the door.

Waving his cast clad arm at the waitress, Truman hollered: "Can we get some pie over here?"

The Ferman boys were playing soccer in the middle of the street as Lee coasted the bike home. Jodi and Ryan Ferman were vicious tweens fond of torturing frogs and blowing things up with firecrackers. Ryan kicked the ball hard, aiming for Lee while Jodi egged him on. Ducking the projectile, Lee pushed on until he was out of the range of fire. One of the Fermans, probably Jodi, hollered after him, calling him a 'fag'.

Pushing through the side door, Lee noted the time on his phone and wondered if he had missed dinner again. He'd hoped to prod his old man for more details about the sale of the farm to Big Bill Daggett.

"Mom," he called out, going up three steps to the kitchen. "Did you make dinner yet?"

No response. No smell of cooking in the air. The radio was on, blaring out some old rockabilly tune. Rounding the corner to the kitchen, Lee found his mother was not there. Just a stranger sitting at the kitchen table with his feet propped up and a beer in his hand. Not a stranger, exactly.

"Hello Lee," said Uncle Elvis.

Lee stopped, scanning the hallway and partial view of the living room. Empty. He turned back to the visitor at the table sipping his dad's Moosehead. "What are you doing here?"

"Came to see my favorite nephew."

"Where's mom?"

"She's not home." Uncle Elvis dropped his boots to the floor and pushed the empty chair back. "Sit."

Lee dropped his backpack to the floor and crossed the room, giving his eccentric uncle a wide berth. He opened the refrigerator and retrieved the jug of iced tea. Trying his best to sound casual, he said: "Did mom say where she went?"

Uncle Elvis studied him for a moment without speaking. His eyes were dark and a wry smile played at the corners of his mouth. Reaching into a back pocket, he produced a pearl-handled jackknife and unfolded the blade. The nickel plating flashed in the overhead light.

"I know what you're up to," he said.

Lee felt his heart thump erratically. Forced himself to breathe through the moment. Be cool. "I wish I was up to something."

A bowl of apples sat in the middle of the kitchen table, tiny fruit flies crawling over the red skin. Lee's mom had insisted on having apples on the ready for as long as he could remember. And despite the heat and the fruit flies, she kept up the tradition although no one in the house ever touched the biblical fruit. Except now, as Uncle Elvis chose one apple from the bunch, buffed it against his white T-shirt and proceeded to slice out a wedge of it with his shiny knife.

"Give up on it, son," he admonished. "It's nothing but bad luck."

"I don't know what you're talking about," Lee replied.

"Don't play stupid with me, Lee. It's insulting to both of us. You think you're the first one to go after it?"

Lee kept his mouth shut. He scrambled his brains for a phrase he had heard before. Something about giving a man enough rope to hang himself. The man with the sideburns and slicked hair was in the mood to pontificate, that much was clear. So let him prattle on, let him hang.

Uncle Elvis bit down on the wedge of apple and proceeded to cut another slice. "Your grandfather wasted twenty years of his life chasing after it, digging holes all over creation. It got so bad he was shoveling in his sleep. Jesus, do you remember how Grandma

Traven would talk about that? Grandpa digging in his sleep?"

The kitchen fell silent as Elvis waited on a reply. The clock over the doorway ticked on and on.

Lee blurted out a response. But not a very convincing one. "Like I said, I don't know what you're talking about."

Elvis tilted out of his chair, jerking up on his feet. Easily a head taller than Lee and a seventy pounds above his weight class. There were wrinkles on his uncle's face but his biceps bulged like a potato in a stocking.

"Give it up," he uttered in a growling voice. "It's nothing but misery to anyone fool enough to dig for it."

His uncle stood looming over Lee, popping another wedge of apple into his mouth. The shining blade in his hand was held at belly-level. One quick slash and it would all be over, intestines spilling out over the scuffed floor tiles. Without thinking, Lee took a step back.

"Are you threatening me?"

Elvis wiped the blade against his jeans and folded the knife. "I'm trying to save you a world of hurt." He gripped Lee's hand, pressing the half-cored apple into his palm. "Stay away from the farm. If you don't, the shit's gonna hit the fan."

Lee yanked his hand away, his palm smeared with apple slime. Uncle Elvis gave him a quick wink before clomping to the door in his heavy boots. When the screen door flapped shut, he lowered himself into one of the kitchen chairs. His hands were shaking, his nerves blown to Hell. He was still in that position when his mother bustled into the kitchen minutes later.

"Was that Elvis?" she asked of her son. "I saw his truck roaring out of here."

Diane Traven slung the shopping bags onto the counter. When she saw her son's face, she froze.

"Honey," she said, approaching her son and cupping his cheeks. "What's the matter? You look like you've just seen a ghost."

15

Absent cousins - The King as rival - The tardy treasure seeker - Rotten boards - The quiet loner type - A violent past - A forgotten well - The stink of Hell

STANDING ALONE AT the end of his driveway, Lee felt exposed and vulnerable, and not just from an attack by the vile Fermen brothers. The visit from his uncle had rattled him more than he cared to admit. When he heard the rumble of an oncoming car, he backed up behind the hedge, expecting to see Elvis' beat up truck come up the street. He let out an exasperated sigh when he saw the black Pathfinder cruising toward him.

Truman sat behind the wheel. He nodded and unlatched the rear door. "Get in."

Steering out of the quiet street, they cruised out of town and onto Route Nine. The Pathfinder dipped and thudded over the cracked pavement.

Lee glanced into the backseat. "Jeremy didn't come?"

"I tried to get him to change his mind but he can be an obstinate shit when he wants to be." Truman drove on, turning off the paved road to the dirt one. "What about Zoe?"

"I texted her."

"Yeah? What'd she say?"

Lee looked out at the fields passing by the window. "She didn't reply."

"More for us," said Truman.

Up the long dusty driveway, they drove past the house and Truman parked the SUV behind the barn where it wouldn't be seen from the road. They opened the rear hatch and hauled out their gear. Each had a full backpack, along with the Buccaneer, two spades, and the heavy pick-ax. They set out across the field toward the creek at the far end.

"How much we got left to search?" Truman asked.

"Half an acre maybe. Not much."

"Good. Then it shouldn't take too long."

"It won't go that quick," Lee said. "With just the two of us."

A crow flapped up from the stalks at their approach, cawing out as it wheeled overhead. Two more birds startled and took flight. Listening to their wretched caws, Lee had begun to hate the sight of the blackbirds.

"I had a visit from Uncle Elvis today."

Truman looked at him with genuine surprise. "No shit. How is that crazy old buzzard?"

"He knows what we're up to."

Truman stopped, forcing his cousin to stop also. "What did he say?"

"He told me to give it up. The bastard practically threatened me."

"He's crazy," Truman said with a dismissive sneer. They walked on. The low stone wall came into view and then the stakes they had planted in the ground. The run of twine drooped lazily to the ground, still heavy with dew.

"I think he's looking for it too," Lee stated.

"The buried loot?"

"That's why he warned me off. Same reason he chased us out of the barn that day."

Truman looked down at his shoes. Canvas sneakers, not the best choice for digging but it was too hot for heavy work boots. The toes of his kicks were damp from the weeds. "Whose uncle is he anyway? I doubt the bastard's even related to us."

They dropped their gear at the foot of the stone wall and strode out to the staked run of land until they found the slash of orange spray paint on the ground. They readjusted the stakes in the ground and pulled taut the drooping run of twine before retrieving the tools.

Lee looked out at the remaining sector of ground left to search. "If we hurry, we can cover a good run of this before the sun goes down."

"Check this out," Truman said, reaching into his backpack. He produced a bottle of Jack Daniels. "I liberated it from the old man's stash."

"Won't he notice?"

"Not for a long time. We'll crack it open when we find this thing."

Lee regarded his cousin. Truman's smile seemed genuine and for the first time in a very long while, Lee felt a certain camaraderie with him. They had been close when they were younger, before a certain mean streak had begun to manifest itself in Truman, causing Lee to pull away. But now, with just the two of them heading off into what was probably a complete farce of a plan, Lee was surprised to discover how much he had missed his older, devil-may-care cousin. He was about to say something to that effect when an angry racket drifted up over the plain.

Following the sound, the two of them watched as a vehicle came bounding and dipping across the field toward them. The ATV rumbled up before them and went silent. Jeremy pulled off his helmet and ran a hand through his sweat-dampened hair.

Truman laughed at him. "Change your mind, sweetheart?"

"Michelle was having a shit-fit about something," Jeremy said. "I got the hell out of there."

"I thought you dumped her?" Truman asked.

"So did I." Jeremy set the helmet onto the ATV seat and looked down at the gear. "Have you guys started yet?"

"We're just getting set up," Lee replied, tightening a knot on the twine.

Jeremy took up the metal detector, flicked it on. "Good. I want to a turn using this thing."

"You can go first then," Truman said.

———— ◆ ● ◆ ————

After a brief instruction on how to read the panel display on the Buccaneer, Jeremy set off with the device, sweeping the coil over the ground. The last section of land on their search was an uneven swath of earth that sloped down to the edge of the creek. The weeds were tall and thick here and the coil would tangle in the damp stalks, forcing Jeremy to trample a patch first before he could sweep it properly. After ten minutes of this toil, the fun of metal-detecting evaporated as the task of trampling weeds became a tedious chore.

He wondered if it would be worth his time to drive back to the barn for the scythe and mow down all the weeds first before resuming the ground detecting. A trickle of laughter echoed across the still air and he looked back to where his two cousins were sitting on the stone wall with beers in hand. For a moment, he wondered if the two of them were laughing at him; suckered into doing the dirty work while they sat on their asses. That wouldn't be a surprise for Truman; he was manipulative as the day was long. Lee was a different story. Not as brainy smart as his older cousin, but weird and secretive. A social retard at school with few friends, Jeremy halfway suspected Lee to turn 'Columbine' one day and show up at school with a gun looking to settle some score. He certainly fit the profile; the quiet loner that no one suspected, or even really knew.

Could they even trust Lee? What if this fabled loot was true and they find the lost treasure of this outlaw guy? Who's to say

Lee wouldn't turn on them, slitting their throats and running off with the booty?

The metal detector pinged, piercing his ear with a sharp tone. Jeremy retraced his path to pinpoint the target but the weeds were too thick. Kicking them down, his sneaker butted up against something solid under the foliage. Testing it further, he found a flat length underfoot, too flat to be natural. Setting the Buccaneer aside, he dug his hands into the weeds and felt the flat surface, followed it along to find a hard corner of right angles. Yanking away handfuls of the stalks and weeds, he looked down at a run of boards nailed together to form some kind of platform. The wood was gray and rotting and clearly hadn't been disturbed for a long time. What the hell was it?

"Do you think the old man was serious?"

Leafing through their grandfather's notebook, Lee looked up at Truman. "Grandpa?"

"Uncle Elvis. You think he was serious about his threat?"

"Felt that way. That dude kinda scares me." He half-expected Truman to mock him for his admission but his cousin just tipped back his beer and gazed out across the darkening plain.

"You should be," Truman stated. He turned and looked at his cousin. "You know he's done time, right?"

"For what?"

Truman flashed one of his grins. "Assault. You know the

backroom poker games at the Chilton tavern? Some redneck tried to cheat old Uncle Elvis at the table and the King went total apeshit on the guy. Put him in the hospital."

Lee scratched his head. "When was this?"

"Years ago. My old man told me about it when he was drunk. He also told me it was hushed-up and to keep my mouth shut about it."

"Damn." The air was cooling quickly as the sun went down but it was more than dew that goosed Lee's flesh. It subsided when they heard Jeremy's voice hollering out from the field.

Truman sat up straight. "What's that fool yelling about?"

"He must have found something," Lee said, slipping down off the stone wall.

"Race you!"

They charged into the field but Lee was no sprinter and Truman's long stride had him beat easily. They stood panting before the cousin kneeling in the weeds.

"What'd you find?" Lee wheezed.

"I'm not sure," Jeremy said. His palms were green from yanking out the weeds around his find. A square platform of rotted boards lay uncovered in the foliage.

"What is it?" Truman asked, kneeling down before the flat structure. "Part of a building?"

"I don't think so," Jeremy replied. He got a good grip on the edge of the platform. "The whole thing moves. See? Help me lift it up."

All of them gripped one side and hauled it up. The platform

tilted to one side and tumbled flat onto the weeds. A gaping hole of night lay at their feet, rimmed by a circle of mortared field stones.

"What is it?"

"It's an old well," Truman said. Kneeling at the base of the foundation, he dug a small flashlight from his pocket and aimed the light down the well. A ring of wet stone flared up in the light, fading quickly to the darkness below.

"How far down you think that goes?" Jeremy asked.

Lee scrounged up a small stone and dropped it down the well. A muffled plop was heard as it hit a wet bottom. "Not too far."

Truman nodded at the metal detector. "Can you get a reading with that thing?"

"Too far down," Jeremy answered. "Anybody bring some rope?"

Lee had. He ran back for the nylon cord and they tied it around the handle and lowered the metal detector down into the darkness of the well. The device squelched and whined, sounding out erratic returns.

"It's picking up something down there," Jeremy said.

"Yeah, but what?"

They hauled the Buccaneer back up. Truman peered down into the well and said: "Good place to hide something."

"You think it's down there?"

"Only one way to find out. One of us goes down there."

Lee took a step back as both Jeremy and Truman fixed their gaze on him. "What? Why me?"

"It's your gig, Scooby-Doo," Truman said. "Me and Daphne will lower you down on the rope."

"Are you crazy? I'm not going down there."

"You're the lightest one here," Jeremy said. "It's gotta be you."

There was no denying that one. Jeremy was a hulk and Truman was a wiry mass of long limbs. Lee looked down over the edge of the slimy rock wall. The smell wafting up from below was a sour rank of earth and sulfur.

"What is that fucking smell?"

Truman grinned at him. "Brimstone."

16

Say hello to the Devil - Rope burns - A broken ankle - A surprise from the sediment - Ascent - A dilemma and a compromise - The fourth Musketeer - A new cartography

THE ROPE WAS knotted into a loop large enough for Lee to slip through. Looping it under him, he clambered over the side of the well and let his cousins lower him down. With Jeremy bearing the brunt of the weight, Truman passed the lantern down to the boy in the makeshift harness.

The lantern's metal hoop slipped through Lee's fingers, almost dropping to the darkness below. He looked up at Truman. "My hands are sweaty."

"If you see the devil down there," Truman said, "tell him I said hi."

"Yeah. Real funny."

"You ready?"

"No."

"Lower him down," Truman said.

The round stone wall was slimy with dew, causing Lee's footing to slip as he repelled slowly into the pit. The descent was anything but smooth as the rope would drop suddenly, jerking the spelunker like a bob on a string. When his foot slipped Lee spun in the air until his elbow smacked against the stone.

"Slow down!" he hollered, his voice bouncing around the echo chamber. Fifteen feet down, he looked up at the circle of sky above him. "Hey! Did you hear me?"

The rope jerked again, plunging another foot down and bouncing Lee precariously on the end. The rope was beginning to cut into his ass cheeks as he tried to get a proper footing against the wall. When the rope jerked again, he was in a freefall, tumbling into the clammy abyss of the well.

Aboveground, Jeremy felt his palms become sweaty under the pull of the rope. His slight-framed cousin dangling on the other end was heavier than he looked. The strain from the rope was beginning to burn his hands and he wished he had brought gloves. Frustratingly, Truman was being no help whatsoever, leaning over the side of the well to watch the descent.

"Grab the rope, asshole!" Jeremy snarled. "My hands are slipping."

Coming about, Truman got a grip on the rope as well as he could manage but the bulky cast on his left arm compromised a proper latch on the nylon.

"Pull, for fuck's sakes!" snarled Jeremy.

"I'm trying—"

The rope slipped through Jeremy's burning palm. Truman had latched on but failed to get his footing. The sudden pull yanked him headfirst into the stone rim of the well and the rope snaked away, trailing over the edge.

A terrified cry rose from the black hole, followed by a loud splash. Jeremy and Truman leaned over the rim.

"Lee! LEE!"

"Oh, shit," groaned Truman. "We killed him."

The fall did not kill him but it took a moment to realize that. He was wet, half-submerged in water and his left ankle was burning in pain. The bottom of the well was a silty sludge under two feet of cold water. The lantern was miraculously still lit, bobbing along the surface of the black water. Snatching it up before it was extinguished, the rose of light bloomed over the circular wall of stone. It was a wonder he didn't break his skull open on one of the rocks. Pushing himself up out of the muck, a spark of pain stung up his left leg, forcing him back into the water. Had he broken something? He couldn't tell, unwilling to try and stand again.

The fumes were horrible. The muddy sediment below him, undisturbed for ages, had been roiled and muddied by his fall and now the stench inside the well grew pungent with an acrid sulfur smell. Truman's joke about the devil wasn't that far off the mark. Was the gaseous reek poisonous?

"Shit!" He had forgotten about his phone in the chaos. Digging it out of his back pocket, he tapped the screen but it refused to light up. Hitting the restart button proved useless. The phone was dead.

Voices echoing down the slick walls drew his attention up. He could see his cousins outlined as dark silhouettes against the gloomy sky bent over the rim above.

"Hey!" Truman called down. "You all right?"

"What the hell was that!" Lee roared back. "I coulda been killed!"

"Sorry, man," Jeremy returned. "Truman's a fucking weakling!"

"Fuck you!" Truman shot back. "Lee, are you okay?"

Bracing himself against the stone foundation, Lee rose slowly from the muck. "I think I broke my ankle."

"Can you move it?" hollered Jeremy.

"A little."

"Then it ain't broke."

He tested his left foot against the sandy mud below. It hurt but not as sharp as the first time.

Truman called down again. "What do you see down there?"

Holding the lantern high, Lee called back. "Nothing. Just mud and water."

"Step out of the rope," Jeremy hollered. "I'm gonna send down the metal detector."

The rope had cinched up under Lee's armpits. Wriggling himself free, the rope was withdrawn and came back down with the Buccaneer dangling from its end. Plunging the coil into the water, Lee swept the shifting silt under him but the gauge returned no signal.

"I got nothing," he bellowed.

"There's gotta be something," Truman called down. "Why hide an old well?"

So nobody falls into it, Lee thought. The whole endeavor had been a waste of time. Making one last sweep with the Buccaneer, he felt the coil knock against something solid underwater.

"Hold on," he said. "I got something."

"A signal?" Jeremy bellowed at him.

Lee probed the object with the coil. A solid mass but it registered no signal on the device. Whatever it was, it wasn't metal. He called up the well to the comrades above. "Pull up the metal detector. I'm gonna try and dig it up."

With the device out of his way, Lee took the trowel from his belt and plunged it into the same area until it tapped solid. Holding his breath, he reached down and got his fingers over a round object. With a little force, he plucked it free from its silty bed and lifted it out of the water.

The hollow eye sockets of a skull emerged from an oozing trail of muddy sediment, along with the telltale grin of fleshless teeth. Recoiling from it, he let it go and scrambled for the rope lowering back down to him.

"Pull me up!"

"What is it?"

"Just get me out of here!"

Hooked around his chest and cinched painfully under his

armpits, Lee rose out of the muck and steadied his ascent to the surface. Gripping the rim of the well, he felt two pairs of hands grab him by the belt and haul him over. Tumbling onto solid earth, he looked up to see his cousins gasping for air. Flinging the rope free, Lee backed away from the well and wiped his hands on his jeans to clean them.

"What happened?" Truman asked, watching his cousin compulsively wipe his hands as if they were stained. "What'd you find?"

It took a moment for Lee to slow the hammering inside his chest. He wondered if this is what hyperventilating felt like.

"A skull."

Jeremy gave Truman a side-glance. "Are you sure?"

Lee pointed at the well. "There's a fucking body down there."

"What?" Truman asked quietly. "Like a cow skull?"

"It was a human skull!" Lee wheezed, suddenly afraid that he would cry. "We gotta call the cops. Jesus Christ."

Truman moved closer and gripped his shoulder. "Okay. Just take it easy. Catch your breath."

Jeremy was on his feet, pacing the weeds. "He's right. We gotta call the cops. This is frigging crazy."

"Just chill, dude," Truman said. "Let's not do anything stupid."

"Stupid?" Jeremy spat. "We are way past stupid at this point. We need to get out of here. Now!"

"We're not done here."

Lee snapped his head up. "You want to keep looking? We just found a body."

"That's not our concern," Truman reasoned. "That could be anybody down there. An accident. Hell, that's probably why they covered the damn thing up. So nobody else would fall down it."

Jeremy's eyes bugged from their sockets. "So what, we just leave it down there?"

Truman was on his feet, keeping his tone even to calm them down. "Of course we'll call the cops, but not until we're done. If we call them now, we'll have to wait weeks before we can come back here again."

The crickets chirped around them. Lee took a breath as his heart slowed. "The property will be sold off by then."

"Exactly," Truman agreed. "Now whoever is down that well has been there a long time. Another day or two won't matter. When we're done here, we make an anonymous call to the cop shop. Agreed?"

Jeremy still didn't like it but Truman went over the argument again, point by point, until he wore the hockey player down.

Jeremy looked out over the patch of land sloping toward the creek. "There's not a lot of land left to search. If it's not down the well, maybe it's not here. The whole thing is a hoax."

Lee had scooped up a handful of dirt, scouring his palms with the grit, unable to shake the feeling that his hands were contaminated. "Or somebody beat us to it a long time ago. Which is probably how Mr. Bones ended up at the bottom of the well."

"You sound like you're giving up," Truman noted, with no small scorn to his tone.

"I'm not giving up," Lee said, brushing the dirt from his hands.

"I just want to go home and take a shower."

Dusk had fallen over the landscape. The trees in the distance were black smudges against the lowering sky but now a light in the distance was bobbing from across the field. An intruder.

"What now?" Jeremy groaned.

"Shit," Lee exclaimed, shooting to his feet. "It's him."

"Who?"

"Elvis."

The flare of the flashlight continued to bob along as it came closer, blinding the eyes of the three young men, their faces bald with guilt.

"We should run," suggested Jeremy.

"Too late for that," Truman replied. "He's already seen us."

Unable to bear the tension anymore, Lee hollered at the intruder. "Who's there?" He felt silly the moment he uttered the words though.

The lightbeam floated forward until it tilted up, flaring under a chin.

"Boo!" she said.

"Goddamn it, Zoe!" Truman barked, turning away in disgust.

"Ha!" Zoe laughed. "You should see your faces!"

"Not cool, Zee," Jeremy grunted. "We thought you were Uncle Creepy."

"Relax, ladies." Zoe came up alongside them, taking in the gaping maw of the open well. "What's this?"

Lee ran a hand through his wet hair. "I thought you quit on us."

"You thought wrong," she said. She trained the flashlight over Lee and his soaked clothes and then down into the darkness of the well before her. "Tell me you didn't go down there?"

A brief glance was exchanged between the three boys but no one volunteered information about the surprise Lee found at the bottom of the well. An awkward moment of silence later, Lee said: "It's not down there."

"It's not anywhere," Truman announced, waving a hand over the patch of land leading to the creek. "We swept the place. There's nothing here."

Scrounging a small stone from the ground, Zoe dropped it down the well, listening for the plop of water. "I'm not surprised," she said.

"The hell does that mean?"

She looked up at the trio. "There's a parcel of land we didn't even know about."

Lee stopped shivering. "What are you talking about?"

"Where's the map?"

Truman fetched their grandfather's map from the backpack and handed it to her. Zoe unfolded it on the ground and shone the light over the grid system that Grandpa Traven had penciled. "There was something odd about this map but I couldn't figure it out at first. See here where the property line of the farm goes all the way down to the creek?"

Lee followed her finger as it traced the boundary line to the winding turn of the creek. "What about it?"

"Look here," she said, tracing her finger to the opposite side of the creek. "The property line of the Traven farm extends to the other side of the creek. Not much, just a meter or two running parallel to the farm on the other side. That's what didn't make sense to me."

"You're losing me, Zee," Truman said. "So the property includes a slice of creek bank on the other side? So what?"

"The creek forms a natural border, so the property line should end there. But the fact it extends beyond it had me puzzled. So I went down to the county clerk's office and dug up some more property maps. Really old ones."

Shrugging her backpack to the ground, she reached inside and pulled out three photocopied pages and laid them over the map.

"This is a copy of a much older map, dated around 1901," she continued, pointing out a squiggly line of calligraphy in the corner of one of the photocopied pages. "The guy at the clerk's office was not pleased since I was making him dig through the archives for it. It shows the lots and concessions of the time. Here's the Traven farm, with the usual boundaries, but look here, at the creek."

They crowded in to see what she was pointing at. The Traven property extended past the creek to enclose another two acres on the far side.

"That used to be part of the farm?" Lee asked. "Why don't we know about it?"

"That part took some more digging," Zoe replied. She pointed to the mystery acreage. "This part of the land had been leased to the county since 1872. Later it was sold off to the township in 1905."

"What's this?" Jeremy enquired, pointing to a matrix of tiny cross hatches on the mystery land. "These little X marks."

"That's the reason the township leased the land from the Traven family in the first place. Those tiny crosses represent a graveyard."

"A graveyard?" Jeremy sputtered, looking past the creek to the stand of trees rising from the other bank. "You're shitting me. There's no graveyard back there."

"There is," Lee confirmed. "It's hidden back behind those trees."

"It started off as a family plot for the Travens but other people started using it," Zoe stated. "That's why the township bought the land. But after World War One, the lot was full and the township closed it down and started another cemetery closer to town."

Truman was nodding his head slowly, taking it all in. "Did Grandpa even know about this?"

"I doubt it," she said. "Since it's not part of the grid on his map. He never looked there."

Lee had the metal detector in hand and was already marching across the scrub to the creek without another word.

"Whoa," Jeremy called out. "Where are you going?"

"Bring the spades," Lee hollered without looking back.

Truman and Zoe gathered up the lantern and shovels, following Lee. Jeremy snatched Truman's arm. "Are you frigging mental or something? No way are we searching a graveyard."

"Then stay here." Truman pulled his arm away and ran to catch up.

Jeremy's face darkened as he stood his ground. When he heard the others splash through the creek, he grabbed the pick-ax and ran after them. "This is fucking retarded," he muttered to no one but himself.

17

A forgotten Necropolis - Eroded sandstone - The wrong
Traven - A correction of relevant dates - Dogs in the night -
The right Traven - Blistered hands and low spirits - The
problematic nature of legends - Robin Hood

THE RASPBERRY BRAMBLES on the far side of the creek bank
were thick and prickly, tearing at their clothes and hands as the
quartet of fortune seekers pushed through. Beyond the brambles
stood a copse of spruce trees with a thick carpet of dry needles
underfoot. Trampling through the brush, they emerged into an
open space surrounded by a wall of trees on every side.

"Holy shit," Truman said, trailing the flashlight beam over the
forgotten cemetery. The sandstone grave markers tilted at
different angles in the swaying bunchgrass, pushed hither and yon
by years of exposure and neglect. Some of the tombstones had
broken in half, leaving jagged edges rising from the earth, and
others had toppled flat to the ground.

The four of them moved through the graves, lantern held high, flashlights bouncing off the broken headstones.

"This place is huge," Truman said.

"It's frigging creepy is what it is," Jeremy announced. He lingered near the tree line, unwilling to venture any further.

Zoe swept her flashlight across the neglected cemetery. "More than an acre. It'll take a couple days to sweep it all with the metal detector."

"We should go back for the stakes and twine," Truman added. "Set up a grid search."

Lee dropped to one knee before a tilting headstone. He brushed at the lichen-crusted to the stone, trying to decipher the eroded inscription. "Forget that. We don't need them."

"This is nuts, man," Jeremy protested. "Let's get out of here."

"Man up," Truman sneered. "Afraid someone's gonna jump out of their grave and get you?"

"Fuck you."

"Shut up," Lee said, rising to his feet. "Everyone spread out. Check the names on the tombstones."

Zoe swung the light in his direction. "For what?"

"Anyone named Traven."

The quiet graves lit up in the bouncing lights as the four of them fanned out across the cemetery. Hands brushed away the grit and lichen to reveal the inscriptions on the stones before moving on. A cabal of forgotten surnames flashed in the lantern light like Smithie, Dobbs, and Balderston. The further they worked their way into the grave, the more bizarre the names became. There was a Brocklehurst and a Grummidge, alongside a Primbleshock and a Cahalabone. Some of the headstones were simply illegible, forcing the searchers to simply count the faded letters to find a match for the Traven surname.

Truman cursed and moved on to another stone. He looked at Zoe, two stones over. "Hey," he said. "You ever hear of gold fever?"

"What about it?" Zoe asked, wiping her palm across another length of sandstone.

"I think our cuz has caught a bad case of it."

Zoe turned to where Truman was pointing. Lee was darting from tombstone to tombstone like it was a race to the finish, scouring each stone and scurrying on.

"He's just like that."

Truman looked at her. "What is it with you two? Always so spastic around each other?"

"You smoke too much dope." She moved on to another headstone.

"You're evading the question," Truman said. He swept his flashlight over the expanse of listing gravestones. "Like this place. All the times I've been out here on the farm, I never knew about this cemetery. But you and Lee knew about it? What's with the secrecy?"

Zoe traced her fingers along a weathered inscription. "Are you gonna keep looking? We got a lot of ground to cover here."

Truman moved on but before he could kneel to inspect another grave, Jeremy was hollering across the cemetery. The other three took off at a sprint to the glow of his flashlight.

"What is it?" Lee blurted out.

"I found a Traven," Jeremy said, shining his light on the stone before him. The others crowded around to read the carved letters. Estelle Harriet Traven, 1844 - 1856.

"This is it," he gushed, proud of his find.

"Close," Lee concluded, shaking his head. "But no cigar."

"What the hell are you talking about? It's a Traven like you asked for."

"It's too early. Before Jesse James was even around."

The hockey player looked ready to fight, his jaw muscles tensing. "Then what time period are we looking for?"

"Anytime after the Civil War, up to the time of his death," Lee said. "Like 1880."

"1882," Truman corrected.

"Right," Lee replied, through a slight gritting of his molars. Seeing the downturn on Jeremy's face, he patted him on the shoulder. "Good find, though. Means we're getting warmer."

Truman, Zoe, and Jeremy turned slowly to their task while Lee scrambled back to the last tombstone he'd inspected, stopping to check the name again before moving on. He knew that it wasn't a race but a queer sense of urgency kept his heart hammering against his ribcage. He wanted to be the one to find it.

The night air was still and sticky with humidity. Above the constant trilling of the crickets, sounds carried clear across the plain. The low hum of a distant vehicle far away, an owl hooting softly. When the snap of a dog barking broke the stillness, they all froze and looked up, fearful they had been found out.

"It's just the Hendershot's mutt," Jeremy said dismissively.

Zoe exhaled. "Jesus. It sounded so close."

"That stupid dog barks at everything. I don't how the Hendershots sleep at night."

They bent back to their task but the unquiet remained, tangled up in their nerve endings like dry rot infesting wood. The hour dragged on and, in the end, it was Zoe who hollered out first. Rushing to her location with the others, Lee felt a twang of envy burn his gut, half-hoping she was wrong.

"I think this is it," she said, looking up at her fellow treasure seekers as they crowded around her.

Lee scrutinized the tombstone before them but the inscription had eroded to barely discernible grooves in the stone. "Are you sure? I can't even read that."

"Here, angle the light on it." Sweeping her palm across the sandstone, she aimed her flashlight against it in such a way as to sharpen the shadows of the weathered inscription. Letters filtered through, followed by a series of numbers:

ALBERT WALKER TRAVEN

1871 - 1880

"The date matches up," Truman said, his tone cut with a sweaty urgency. "Two years before James was killed."

For the second time this night, Lee bristled at his cousin's knowledge of the notorious outlaw. He wished, in fact, that Truman and Jeremy had never stuck their noses into this business in the first place. It should have been just him and Zoe. This four musketeer routine was starting to chafe.

"Jesus, look at those dates," Jeremy said, adding his light to Zoe's to enhance the shadow relief. "Just a kid. Nine years old."

"Where's the metal detector?" Lee demanded, twitching his attention from one to the next until Truman brought the Buccaneer. "Sweep this area."

Truman turned the device on and waved the coil end over the weed-choked grave. All became still, listening for a telltale beep that never came.

"Nothing," Truman said.

"It's too far down for the detector to reach," Zoe said, sweeping her hair from eyes. "How deep did they dig graves back in the nineteenth century? Six feet?"

"Time to find out," Lee snapped. Snatching up the spade, he plunged the blade into the hard earth and kicked it down hard with his heel. "Look out."

Jeremy lashed out, knocking Lee backward. "Are out of your mind? We are not digging up a fucking grave, man!"

Lee clung to the shovel, swinging it back like a weapon. "Get the fuck off me. Swear to God, I will knock your brains in."

Zoe and Truman rushed between them like referees, arms stretched out to separate the combatants, shaming them both into disarmament.

"He's right," Zoe said, edging closer to Jeremy. "This is going too far."

To his surprise, Truman edged toward Lee's orbit. "So what

now? We walk away after all this?"

Each side groped for a solution to the impasse but all came up short, choking on a dearth of paths forward. Lee let the shovel drop. Taking a stride forward, he sunk the tip of the spade back into the earth and looked Jeremy clean in the eye.

"You want to take the high road, then leave," he growled. He turned the first clod of soil. "You want to get rich, then you get your hands dirty. Simple as that."

Lee kept digging, pushing the blade down into the hard-packed earth and tilting out solid clumps of dry soil. His eyes remained fixed on Jeremy as he pushed and grunted against the earth.

Jeremy glowered for a moment before he took a step back. Truman, grinning like an ape again, pressed the advantage and thrust the pick-ax into his cousin's hands.

Jeremy hung his head as if already condemned, and then he swung the pick, driving it deep into the parched soil.

The earth piled up beside the old grave site, dappled with the sweat of the diggers as they took turns with the spade. Lee dug with a fevered mania until he stood chest deep in the ground, his palms blistered and bleeding. When the shovel handle became too slick from his own blood, he crawled out of the pit and rolled onto his back. "Somebody else dig for a while."

Jeremy, sitting with his back against a headstone, watched the others turn to look at him. As the biggest and strongest of the quartet, the task naturally fell to him but he shook his head. "Don't look at me. I am not digging anymore."

"I'll do it," Zoe said, even though her palms throbbed with blisters.

Lee waved her off. "Truman, get your ass down there."

"No can do," Truman replied, raising his left arm. "Can't dig with this thing."

The eldest cousin had begged off the hard labor because of the cast on his left arm. Undue exertion risked straining the bone, he'd claimed.

"I don't care." Sheened with sweat, Lee's face shone in the lantern glow. "Do your part. You can heal later."

Scolded, Truman dropped into the open pit and took up the spade. Zoe uncapped her water bottle and handed it across to Lee. He poured a little over his face before taking a swig.

"You okay?" she asked, taking back the water bottle.

"I'm a mess," he said, holding up his bloodied palms.

"Hold out your hands," she said. When he complied, she poured cold water over the blisters.

"Thank you." He watched her twist the cap back onto the bottle. Her frame shuddered under a shiver. "You cold?"

She peeled at the T-shirt clinging to her skin. "The damp is setting in."

Lee hooked Truman's backpack and dragged it closer. He rummaged up the bottle of Jack Daniels and handed it to her. "This'll help."

"Hey!" Truman protested. "I'm saving that for when we find

this thing."

"Close enough," Lee said, nodding at the excavated grave. "Keep digging."

Zoe took a pull on the bottle and handed it back.

"Better?"

"Yes," she said. "Thank you."

Lee twisted around to where Jeremy sat back against a headstone. "Jay, you cold?"

"Freezing."

Watching the others drink his booze, Truman scowled and cursed as he flung dirt out of the pit. A low rumble of complaints issued from his gritted teeth, punctuated by each stab into the ground. "Stupid fucking...Jesse James...and his stupid...fucking treasure."

Jeremy took an extra pull on the bottle before handing it back. Watching Truman dig, he said: "What's the big deal with Jesse James anyway? Why's he so famous and shit?"

"He was an outlaw," Lee replied. "Like Robin Hood, stealing from the rich and giving to the poor. You know, sticking it to the man."

Jeremy shrugged. "Cool."

Truman stood panting in the pit. "That's bullshit," he said.

"What's bullshit?"

"That Robin Hood garbage," Truman said. "He didn't steal from the rich and he sure as shit didn't give it to the poor."

Lee shook his head. "He struck back at the establishment, robbing banks and stuff."

Truman rested his cast-clad arm on the end of the spade. "Who's money do you think was in those banks? Dirt poor farmers who scraped together a few measly dollars as their life savings. And in swoops Jesse fucking James, who steals it all and everybody thinks he's some hero?" He took up the spade and continued to dig. "He was a thief and a murderer."

Lee wasn't having any of it. "That's your opinion."

"No, that's history," Truman retorted. "Try doing some actual research, Lee, instead of relying on some kid's book."

"Whatever," Jeremy scoffed, dismissing the whole idea. "Dude's dead. What does it matter?"

"Of course it matters," Zoe replied. "You want to know the truth, not just some silly legend. Legends aren't real."

"Then what the hell are we doing here?" Jeremy countered, pointing at the partially exhumed grave. He regarded his companions with their blistered hands and sweaty brows, the graveyard dirt crusted under their fingernails.

And then the spade bit loud into something solid.

The others scrambled forward. Truman was on his knees, scraping the dirt away with the broad pan of the shovel. A length of blackened wood emerged from the raw earth.

"Bingo," he gloated.

Slipping the trowel from his belt, Lee dropped into the pit and began to dig, crowding out his cousin.

"Get outta the way, man," Truman complained.

"Shut up and dig."

18

A casket of hardwood - Paper shrouds and dry bones - Unshod feet of the dead - Wells Fargo - Double eagles - Schofield - Wet powder and dry cartridges - Bang bang - Just like Jesse James

THE COFFIN WAS small. Four feet in length with a span half that. The earth had been dug around its edges to expose the entirety of it to the night air. The wood of the casket was stained almost black from over a century in the ground but the lid did not crumble under the abuse of the spade. A hardwood like oak or maple, unusual for the construction of a modest coffin.

Truman stood at the crown while Lee manned the opposite end of the open pit. Zoe and Jeremy looked down from above. None of them took their eyes from the small casket.

"Still pretty solid," Lee said, knocking the handle of his trowel against the coffin lid.

Truman ran his fingers along the edge, looking for the seam.

"Built to last."

Lee tugged but the lid held fast. He tilted his gaze up to Zoe. "There's a pry bar in my backpack."

When Zoe handed the tool down, Jeremy gripped her arm to stop her. He searched the eyes of each of his cousins and said: "Are we really gonna do this?"

No one moved. From far away down the plain came the mindless barking of the Hendershot's dog.

Lee took the pry bar from Zoe's hand and stabbed it into the seam of the casket lid. Straining as he hauled back until the lid cracked open, flinging him into the dirt wall. Truman wedged the spade into the seam and together they pried the lid up. A stained, worm-eaten shroud covered the remains underneath. Truman trailed up one corner of the material and flung it back.

The dry bones of the child lay collapsed within the narrow slot of coffinwood, the small skeletal hands folded piously over the sunken breastplate. The clothes had desiccated to a papery husk that hung draped over the fretwork of the ribcage. The dark void of the eye sockets stared up at them. Four teeth were missing.

Jeremy turned away but Lee could not tear his gaze from the dwarf-like skeleton, scanning down the length of the remains to where the brittle bones of the small feet lay scattered in the bottom of the wooden box. There were no shoes but nestled below the skeleton's feet were three heavy canvas sacks.

"Holy shit."

The others held their breath as Lee reached down to brush away the gritty sand that had settled over one of the satchels. Two words printed onto the material became legible. *WELLS FARGO.*

"Get it out of there," Truman hissed.

The canvas bags were heavy and they slurred with a tinkling sound as the pair in the grave hoisted them to the cousins topside. As Truman and Lee scrambled out of the hole, Jeremy unfolded a jackknife and cut away the corded end of one of the bags.

Money spilled onto the bare ground. Stacks of American banknotes, antique and brittle, were bound in paper bands. Alongside the Yankee currency lay bundles of British pound notes, French francs, and Mexican pesos.

The eyes of the four adventurers bulged from their sockets.

"Oh my God."

"How much is there?"

Zoe lifted out a stack of bills and fanned her thumb against the end. The dry paper crumbled, disintegrating into confetti before their eyes.

"It's rotten," she said. She tested a stack of pound sterling, but it crumbled as quickly as its American brethren. "It's all rotten."

The breeze had picked up, scooping through the trees around them and scattering the shreds of money through the crabgrass.

"Fuck me," said Truman, watching it blow away.

Clawing at the drawstrings of another satchel, Lee tore open the canvas and something glinted in the play of the flashlight. He tipped it out, spilling coins of different sizes onto the dusty ground. Double eagles and half-eagles tinkled under his fingertips, all of it gold, all of it dating from the Reconstruction era.

Mouths gaped open. When Lee raised his eyes to meet his cousin's, the grin on his face looked gleefully unhinged.

"It's real."

"We're rich," stammered Jeremy. "Jesus Christ, we're rich!"

Hooting and gibbering, the foursome danced around their prize like deranged acolytes of some pagan cult, their legs scissoring through the glow of the dropped flashlights. Forgotten in the bliss were the bleeding blisters and aching muscles, the recriminations of the previous days and the dry bones of a dead child in the desecrated grave.

They collapsed into the dirt and the bottle was trotted out, passed around. They put their lips to it, already drunk on the prize sprawled before them.

Gimlet-eyed, Truman studied the coins. "How much you think is there?"

Jeremy took up a coin and turned it to the light. "This says twenty dollars."

"That's just the face value," Zoe said, reaching for one of the double eagles. "And that was in 1875. The gold alone is worth a hell of a lot more."

"Anybody know the price gold now?"

"Over a grand an ounce," Truman replied.

"And we still got another sack of it here," Lee said, hauling up the third, unopened bag. Untying the strings, he reached inside but his brow suddenly furred. "There's something else in here."

He withdrew a bundle wrapped in oilcloth and laid it on the ground. Peeling back the oily material revealed an enormous revolver with a long barrel of gunblack metal and a grip piece of burled walnut. A lethal instrument of firepower not used in over a century.

"Jesus, look at that thing," said Jeremy. " Let me see it."

Lee handed it across and Jeremy tested the weight of it in his hand. "It's heavy. Feel that, Zee."

She took the weapon from him, gripping it stout in both hands. "Why is it here?"

The outsized weapon looked even bigger in her small hands. Lee was grinning again. "You know what that is?"

"A gun?" Sarcasm frosting her reply.

"It's a Smith and Wesson," Lee said. "Schofield model."

"Weapon of choice of one Jesse James," added Truman.

Jeremy regarded the two of them with disdain. "Are you two having a geekgasm?"

Truman held out his hand. "Pass it here."

Zoe handed the gun over and wiped her hands. "It's all oily."

"To preserve it," Truman said. Pulling a red paisley handkerchief from his back pocket, he began wiping down the gun metal. "Whoever buried the loot planned to use this again."

They watched him clean the piece, wiping the oil away with the handkerchief. Testing his thumb against the top sight, the revolver broke open on its hinge with the cylinder and barrel tucking down. Twisting the material into each bore of the cylinder, he jerked the gun up, snapping the barrel closed with a sharp click. Cleaned of oil and buffed dry, the black metal flashed brilliantly against the false light.

"It's heavy but it's balanced nicely," he said, aiming the weapon at an imaginary target. "Fucking beautiful piece, you ask me."

Lee reached back into the satchel and produced two small boxes stamped with fine print on the cover. "Damn," he exclaimed, plucking the lid from one of the containers. "There's bullets too."

Opening the other box, Truman shook the cartridges into his palm. The patina on the copper casing was dull but otherwise looked normal. "These look half-decent," he said. "What are the chances these will still fire?"

Lee held one up to the light. "I dunno. It's over a hundred years old. The gun'll probably blow up in your hand."

"Then we'll let Jay try the first round."

Jeremy frowned, which made Lee laugh. Thumbing the lever, he broke the gun and fitted six rounds into the cylinder. A weird tingle ran up Lee's arm as he snapped the gun closed.

"That's a really dumb idea, guys," Zoe said. "Someone's going to hear it."

"Way out here?" Truman replied. "Hell, the damn thing probably won't even fire."

"Pass it up," Jeremy said.

Truman handed the weapon over while Lee took one of the empty beer cans and set it atop a tombstone. Jeremy gripped the heavy gun with both hands, drew aim at the can and fired.

Nothing happened.

"It's stuck," Jeremy said.

"You gotta cock it." Truman gripped the barrel and thumbed

back the hammer until it clicked. "Try it now."

Jeremy steadied his aim and braced for the kick. A fizzling sound whistled from the cylinder when he pulled the trigger, followed by a whiff of smoke but no blast.

"Dud," Truman said. "My turn."

The Schofield came up again as Truman steadied it with both hands, held his breath and pulled the trigger. Loud as a thunderclap, issuing a cloud of sour gunsmoke in the air. Everyone but the shooter had ducked at the report. When the smoke cleared, the beer can sat untouched on the stone.

"That," said Truman, "was fucking epic."

"Give it here," Lee said. He took the heavy pistol in one hand and drew the barrel up to the target.

"Two hands, Lee," warned Truman. "That thing's got a hell of a kick."

"No way. This is how Jesse James did it, man." Lee closed one eye, squinting the other as he drew aim. Then he whispered: "Just like Jesse James."

The load fired and the recoil kicked the gun violently straight into Lee's brow. He staggered back, tripped over the spade and fell flat on his ass. The pistol tumbled from his hand, clattering against the metal detector. The others ducked, expecting the damn thing to go off.

Cursing, Lee touched the hot sting on his brow. When he pulled his hand away his fingers were red with blood.

19

Recoil - The smell of charred currency - Victory soured - Dividing the spoils - Back across the creek - Headlights in the fog - The local constabulary - Interring the evidence - Another pledge

TRUMAN HOVERED OVER the downed shootist, his grin beaming. "Nice job, Rambo."

"I'm bleeding," Lee stammered, looking at his bloodied fingertips.

"You're an idiot," Truman replied. Retrieving the gun, he opened it at the hinge and shook out the cartridges. "I told you that thing had a kick."

Jeremy howled at him. "You're such a fucking loser, Lee. Seriously."

Zoe pushed past them. "You guys are assholes, you know that?"

"Is it bad?" Lee asked her, still dabbing at the cut.

"It's just a nick, for Christ's sakes," Jeremy groaned. "Tape it up and tough it out."

Lee scowled. "Thanks, coach. But I forgot my first-aid kit."

Zoe dug a crumpled tissue from her pocket and applied it to his brow. "Put pressure on that. It'll stop bleeding in a minute."

Sitting across from the spilled bags of money, Truman watched her minister to the gash on their cousin's brow. He scrutinized her gentleness and cooing tone and something about the tableau rankled him. Turning away, he dug into his backpack and came away with his brass Zippo lighter. The lid popped open with a satisfying click and he struck the flame. He had altered the lighter, allowing the cloth wick to extend high out of its cage. The inverted teardrop of flame was almost five inches high. He reached down to the pile of paper currency on the ground and selected one stacked bundle. The edges of the bills were badly frayed and he tossed it back in favor of a more pristine stack of antique currency.

"Truman," Zoe said when she smelled something burning. "What are you doing?"

The stack of brittle twenty dollar bills burned quickly in Truman's hand, giving off a greasy black smoke. The fire reflected bright in his mesmerized eyes.

Lee sprang up. "Are you crazy?"

"This shit is worthless. Except maybe as a museum piece." Truman turned the stack of burning money in his hand until it threatened to burn his fingers. He let it fall onto the tumble of paper currency.

"It's money!" Jeremy barked as he pushed the smoldering stack away from the others. "These are hundred dollar bills."

Amused, Truman popped the brass lighter open and shut. "Where you gonna cash a hundred-year-old C-note? You think the Seven-Eleven's gonna take that?"

"Doesn't mean you just burn it, you arsonist," Lee spat. "We found the lost treasure of Jesse James. We'll be famous."

Truman snapped the lighter shut. "You can't tell anyone about this. Not a single fucking soul." He searched the eyes of the other two. "None of us can."

Lee stammered. "Are you nuts?"

"Take a look around, cuz. We just desecrated a grave. Cops don't take kindly to that shit." He wagged his chin at the spill of gold coins at their feet. "And if they got wind of this, the town would just take it away from us."

"Bullshit," Jeremy protested.

Lee's mouth was moving, trying to form a counter-argument when Zoe spoke up. "He's right," she said. "We're not on the farm. This is public property."

Truman was grinning again. "Ergo, if a word of this gets out, we are all fucked."

The cousins fell silent as the truth settled in like an infection. The dog on the Hendershot's farm had finally stopped barking.

"So this was all for nothing," Jeremy said, turning away in disgust. "Great job, Lee. Fucking stellar."

"There's still the gold," Lee replied.

"Aye, captain," Truman croaked in a bad pirate's growl. "There's still yar gold."

A degree of disdain fell from Jeremy's gaze. "Then let's divvy it up and get out of here."

When he dropped to one knee and reached for the coins, Lee gripped his arm. "Hold on. It's not that simple."

"It couldn't be any simpler, stupid. We split it four ways. Equal shares."

"You all laughed at me for this, remember? Equal shares isn't right."

Truman's eyes narrowed. "So what, you get a bigger cut?"

"I earned it."

"My ass you did," barked Jeremy.

Lee's teeth gritted as he spoke. "This was my idea. You two coat-tailed the whole ride."

"No way," Jeremy shot back. He snatched up a handful of the gold, letting the coins spill through his fingers. "This is our inheritance. The parental units can squabble over the real estate but this, this is ours."

Truman leaned forward. "We quarter it. Equal shares all round."

Zoe, silent during this whole exchange, watched as the three of them turned to her. Waiting for her call. She looked at Lee. "They're right, Lee. It has to be equal shares."

Trumped, Lee looked away. "Fine."

"But not here," Zoe said, rising to her feet. "Let's get it back to the barn. We can divide it up there."

The heavy Wells Fargo bags were lashed together and slung over the shoulders of the three boys. They gathered up the tools and fought through the thicket to get back to the Traven property. Splashing across the creek, Zoe stopped and cocked a thumb back at the treeline. "Wait. What about the grave?"

"Shit," Jeremy said.

Truman huffed impatiently. "What about it?"

"We have to backfill it," Zoe said. "We can't just leave it like that."

"Who's gonna notice? No one ever goes there."

The cold water swirled around their ankles.

"She's right," Jeremy said. "We can't—"

"Forget it," Truman replied, wading forward to the other side. "This shit ain't getting any lighter."

"We'll come back tomorrow and rebury it." Lee splashed ahead, tugging Zoe's arm. "Come on."

The idea of leaving the child exposed to the elements left her queasy but the others went on, climbing the creek bank. She hurried after them.

The heavy sacks were strapped onto the cargo rack of the quadrunner. Firing it up, Jeremy trundled along slowly while the others gathered up the rest of the gear and started the long walk back to the farmhouse.

Cresting a gentle slope, Jeremy killed the engine, waiting for the others to catch up. A low fog had returned, steaming up the cooling night air.

"What's wrong?" Lee asked when they came alongside the all-terrain-vehicle.

Jeremy looked at Zoe. "Did you leave your headlights on?"

"No."

"Kill the flashlights," Jeremy said. "Now!"

The flashlights went out, the lantern extinguished. "What is it?" Zoe asked.

"Near the barn," Jeremy said, pointing at the fog.

Through the haze glowed twin dots of halogen light. Zoe's station wagon sat dark near the barn but two other vehicles were now parked alongside it. One was a battered pickup truck, the other a patrol car of the Carthage Police Service.

All four cousins ducked.

Truman turned on the others. "Why are the cops here?"

"Uncle Elvis," Lee said, eyes fixed on the battered pickup. "He ratted us out."

"Great," Jeremy fumed. "Now what do we do?"

"Run for it." It was all that Lee could think of.

Zoe snatched his wrist. "My car is sitting right there."

"There's no way they didn't see the ATV," Truman said, his eyes fixed on the police cruiser. "But we can't waltz in there with bags of money."

Lee surveyed the open plain around them. Flat earth in every direction, nowhere to hide. "We have to bury it."

Jeremy turned on him. "Are you retarded? We spent half the night digging it out of the ground."

"Do you see anywhere else to hide it, brainiac?

"We gotta make this quick," Truman whispered. Taking the

spade, he crawled around behind the ATV. "Everybody start digging."

A shallow pit, no more than two feet deep, was all they could manage to excavate. The Wells Fargo bags were freed from the rack and dragged into the hole. Together they shoveled and kicked dirt onto it, backfilling the hole with their fabled trove. Lee stamped the soil underfoot to pack it down and Zoe scattered handfuls of dead weeds over it.

"Done," she said, looking back across the field to the barn. The fog had receded and she could see the dark figures of two men near the vehicles. "Time to face the music."

Truman scanned their position. An indistinguishable spot in a field of knee-high barley. "Hang on. We need something to mark this spot or we'll never find it."

Lee stabbed the spade into the earth, standing it vertically in the ground. "Done."

Zoe pushed it down. "We don't want anyone else to see it."

"Come here," Jeremy said, pulling Lee closer and spinning him around. He dug into Lee's backpack, found the can of spray paint and splattered the earth with Dayglo orange. "There. They won't spot that from the barn."

Lee stuffed the can back into his pack. "Okay, that's the best we can do. First chance we get, we come back for it."

"Not so fast," warned Truman. "We need something more."

Jeremy growled, impatient with all of them. "What do you want, a prayer?"

"A promise," Truman replied. "That none of us sneak back here and runs off with it."

Scorn passed over Zoe's features. "Jesus, Truman. Don't be so paranoid."

He regarded her. "You haven't dealt with cops much, have you?"

Zoe kept mum. Truman was the authority on that subject and they all knew it.

He went on, nodding at the police car in the distance. "That cop isn't just passing by. God knows what kind of trouble we're in for. I need a vow from each of you that nobody sneaks back here without the others."

Jeremy frowned at the implication. "Dude, we're family."

"Exactly."

The ensuing silence was broken by a flash of harsh light coming from the direction of the barn. The police officer on scene was sweeping the empty field with a powerful searchlight. The flare of light lingered over the ATV.

Lee rose to his feet, exposing himself to the floodlight. "All right. I swear to God I won't screw you guys over."

"Me, too," said Zoe, stretching up to stand alongside Lee.

Truman eyeballed the last of the quartet to submit. Jeremy stood, hating every moment of being blackmailed by his own kin. "Yeah, yeah," he muttered. "I swear."

"That makes four," Truman said.

The co-conspirators shared a brief glance before marching toward the barn, all of them caught in the glow of the searchlight.

20

Sticker generation - Stolen property - Inevitable denial - Laying charges - The station house - A story agreed upon - The man in the sideburns gloats - A reckoning - An unwanted family reunion

OFFICER PHIL CARSON had joined the Carthage Police Services after first working in the city. Born and raised in Shelburne, he had always wanted to live in a larger metropolis but, after three years as a beat cop, he found the city distasteful and moved back home. The pace suited him better but he was bewildered and how he was treated by old friends and neighbors. Everyone was polite and friendly, but they kept their distance. It was as if they didn't trust him now that he was a police officer. Or, he mused, they didn't trust themselves. He'd made peace with it but on occasion, it still irked him.

There was one exception, an old friend since childhood who had harbored a strange fascination for the King of rock and roll.

But then Elvis had always been a strange duck. Like any town, theirs had its stratified class system but Elvis seemed to float outside of it all, moving between the country club set on the nicer side of town and the grittier class of the trailer park on the other side of the train tracks.

And everyone, including Officer Phil, called him Uncle Elvis. As if the man was a distant relation to all and sundry in their little town.

"The problem," Elvis said, leaning against the side of his truck, "is the lack of corporal punishment. The moment that's withdrawn is when all of society begins circling the toilet bowl."

Officer Phil glanced at his watch again, silently bemoaning the late hour. "I hear it all the time. Kids today are out of control, running wild and what-have-you."

"It's a matter of consequences," Elvis said, kicking a stone across the yard. "If a kid knows he's gonna get a beating, he acts straight. He's learned, and I mean deep down learned, the fundamental law of the universe."

"Which is?"

Elvis scratched at his belly. "Cause and effect. That every action is met with reaction and every decision carries consequence."

"You don't think it's just a matter of perception?" Officer Phil asked. "Every generation looks at the younger one and thinks the world's going to hell in a handbasket. But I don't think they're any worse than we were at that age."

"We'll have to agree to disagree," the King replied. "You and me, we may have gotten up to some crazy shit when we were young but we always knew there was a limit. And there were consequences. Kids today, they're so mollycoddled they need a gold sticker every time they wipe their ass."

A low noise carried in on the breeze. Officer Phil looked up and nodded at the dark field. "Speak of the devil," he said.

Four youths, aged between 18 and 22, emerged from the low mist like some prehistoric tribesmen cast out of their Neolithic era into the present day. Their faces were grimed with dirty sweat, their clothes wet and torn. They shivered as they came out of the dark, with eyes that darted about nervously like wood mice.

"Well hello there," Officer Phil said, noting their filthy hands and mud-splattered shoes. "Nice night for a stroll."

Lee looked past the police officer to the man with the slicked pompadour. "What's going on?"

"What were you clowns doing out there?" Uncle Elvis asked, wagging his chin in the direction of the open field.

Chary of the uniformed officer, Truman answered for them. "Nothing."

"Your uncle called me because someone broke into the barn here and stole some property." Officer Phil took a step closer, his shoes crunching on the gravel. He took time to look each of them in the eye. "Do you people know anything about that?"

"No," said Lee, presuming to speak for all of them.

Elvis pushed himself away from the truck and approached Lee. "Don't waste the officer's time, son. Where's all the gear?"

When they had walked out of the dark fields, their hands were empty. The shovels and metal detector were hidden under a pile of weeds, well away from the hole they had dug. Lee stood still, trying his level best not to be intimidated by the man towering over him.

"I don't know what you're talking about."

Uncle Elvis studied the young man, waiting for something to crack. He turned and looked at Zoe. "Does he speak for you?"

"It wasn't us," Zoe replied.

The King was equitable in his contempt, ladling it over all of them. "You really want to play it this way?"

Quick side-eyed glances went round between the four youths but none spoke further. Elvis turned to the constable. "Officer, charge these people."

Officer Phil, who had clearly hoped to avoid this exact scenario, sighed wearily. He opened the rear door of his cruiser and waved the group forward. "Climb in everybody. We'll sort this out at the station."

Lee's eyes dished with shock. "You can't be serious."

The man in the sideburns turned on him. "Get in the car."

⟡⟡⟡

The Carthage Police Station was housed in a restored Georgian building of dressed stone and sashed windows under a gable roof. In contrast to the painstaking restoration of the exterior, the interior had been remodeled in the most functional manner possible. The beige walls and gray carpeting rendered the lobby as appealing as an unemployment office. The smell of stale coffee was smudged into every corner.

The four bedraggled treasure seekers sat in hard-backed chairs in the small lobby looking tired but pensive. The big school room clock over the door indicated 4:12 AM.

Zoe picked at the grime under her fingernails. "How long are they going to make us wait?"

"It's a tactic," Truman said. "Making us cool our heels out here, imagining the worst."

"Why?" Jeremy asked.

"To wear us down. When Officer Friendly comes out, he'll be all smiles and kind words, like we're pals. Hoping we'll spill our guts."

Lee peered down the hallway of the small station but saw no one. The place seemed deserted. "What happened to Uncle Creepy?"

"He's probably back there sharing donuts with Phil," Truman said. "I told you that old bastard wants it for himself. The cop's probably in cahoots with him, too."

Jeremy groaned. "Don't start with the conspiracy theories. Please."

Zoe rose from her chair and stretched her back. "Do you think they'll call our parents?"

"Without a doubt."

Jeremy looked ill at the prospect. Zoe began to pace. "I so don't need this right now," she said.

"We need to get our story straight," Lee said. When the other three turned his way, he went on. "They're gonna question us separately. We all have to be on the same page."

Zoe stopped. "What is our story?"

Lee scratched his chin. He had spent the last hour trying to come up with something that didn't sound completely risible. "We wanted to spend one last night at the farm before it's sold off. We made a campfire, had a few beers. That's it."

"Yeah," Jeremy said with a sneer. "That sounds plausible."

"You got a better story?"

A sound to their left made them shut up. Officer Phil appeared in the doorway, waving one of them forward.

"Jeremy?" he said. "Come on in here, please."

The knob of Adam's apple on Jeremy's throat bobbed up and down. He crossed the lobby like a condemned man walking the plank. The police officer put a hand on his shoulder, guiding him into a room and closed the door behind them.

"He's gonna crack," Lee said, his knee tapping uncontrollably.

"No, he won't," Zoe said. "Have some faith."

She and Lee both turned to Truman for his speculation. He leaned back, clunking the hard cast against the seat rail. "Jay isn't good around authority figures. If Officer Friendly talks to him like a coach, he'll fold."

The air in the old police station went flat. Zoe retreated to a chair and Lee tried to keep his knee from bouncing with a spastic energy. The big clock on the wall ticked on.

An hour later, Zoe lay curled up in the uncomfortable chair as the chill from her wet clothes seeped into her bones. Lee stood before the vending machine, searching his pockets for change that wasn't there. Truman sat with his feet up reading a paperback. Where he had gotten it from, Lee had no idea.

"Hey," Lee whispered to Truman. "You got any quarters?"

"Spent 'em all. But I got a sack of gold coins."

"Don't screw around," Lee hissed, glancing over the room for eavesdroppers. The police station seemed as deserted as before.

Zoe opened one eye. "Would you guys shut up, please."

Truman grinned and went back to his book. Lee eyed the single-serving bags of chips behind the glass of the vending machine, locked out of his reach.

A third, gravelly voice boomed through the lobby. "So you found it, huh?" it said.

Uncle Elvis stood in the doorway, leaning up against the jamb. His eyes were creased in a bemused smile, pleased with all he surveyed.

Zoe unfolded herself, alert to trouble. Lee felt the hunger pangs turn sour. Truman kept reading his book but he was the first to address the rockabilly refugee.

"You here to gloat, Uncle Elvis?"

Elvis leaned away from the door frame and eased down into the empty chair between Zoe and Truman but he kept his gaze squared on the young man at the vending machine.

"Told you it was bad luck," he said.

Lee tried to match the iciness of his uncle's stare but fell short. "Why did you have us arrested?"

"Weren't you paying attention? Break and enter. Theft. What was the other one?"

Lee cut him off. "It's Grandpa's barn."

"Yes," Elvis agreed. "But that don't mean you just march in and take what you want. It doesn't belong to you." He waited a moment before continuing. "Where's the stuff you took? The metal detector and the maps?"

Truman closed the paperback. "You're after it too," he said. "Aren't you?"

"Do I look stupid to you, son?"

When Truman didn't reply, Lee broke in. "You want us out of the way."

"I think you been watching too much TV," Elvis said.

The click of a door sounded from the hallway. Jeremy reappeared, escorted by the police officer. His face was drawn, his eyes cast lifelessly at the floor.

"Have a seat, son," Officer Phil said before turning his attention to the only female in the room. "Zoe? Your turn."

Zoe's gaze lit on Lee briefly as she got to her feet. Her pupils were dilated, the irises all dark brown.

"Be cool," he whispered. It was the only thing his frozen brain could grasp, wanting to placate her unease. He watched the officer escort her from the lobby. Jeremy sat quietly in the far chair, his head down and his face drained of color.

"Jay," Lee said to him. "You all right?"

The young athlete didn't even look up.

"I believe the boy's reckoning the consequences of his actions," Uncle Elvis said. Stretching out his long legs, he crossed one scuffed motorcycle boot over the other. "I hear Coach Stanfield is pretty strident about keeping his team clean. One criminal offense and you're out."

Jeremy flinched as if prodded by a sharp stick, but he kept his eyes on the floor and his mouth shut.

Lee had never held much love for his bully cousin but seeing Jeremy so cowed provoked an alien feeling of protectiveness.

"Leave him alone."

"Just making sure your cousin understands the choice he faces."

"Why don't you go to Hell," Lee said. "None of us would be here if it weren't for you."

"You're blaming me for the shit you stepped in?" Uncle Elvis was grinning again, clearly enjoying the parlay. He was about to go on when a sudden ruckus erupted near the front entrance. A number of people were bottlenecking at the door, rushing the police station like a lynch mob.

Elvis' grin broke wide. "Well, what do you know? It's a family reunion."

The color in Lee's face drained away. Jeremy hung his head even lower. Truman, for the first time in the entire night, looked alarmed at the people rushing in. He spoke for them all.

"Shit."

"Where's my son?" barked Jeremy's father.

"Who's in charge here?" demanded Aunt Fran, searching the lobby to find only relations and no police officers on duty. "Where's Zoe?"

Lee was about to respond when his collar was yanked, jerking him to his feet. His father's face was red. "Break and enter?" he snarled at his son. "What the hell is this all about?"

Lee pushed his father's hands away. "Ask Uncle Elvis."

"What?" Grant Traven scanned the room. "Where is he?"

The chairs were all empty. The man in the sideburns had vanished from the police station lobby.

21

The collective claws of Mama and Papa bear - Dissension among the clan - Glazed eyes and guilty looks - Charges laid and not withdrawn - Culpability of the naive

THE PARENTS OF the delinquent four, siblings all, were still smarting from the previous detente over the inheritance of the farm. Already aggrieved, they went at each other with the kind of vehemence that only a protective parent can muster. Officer Sean Garrity had been called in to work early to help process the violators and handle crowd control. The sole authority figure in the room with his uniform and regular-issue sidearm, Officer Garrity was helplessly out of his league in this room of mama bears and papa bears.

Lee sat silently dying a slow death as the parental units barked and flailed their hands. Jeremy and Truman were equally mute, equally mortified. Zoe was still in the little room with the senior officer.

"That is nonsense," shrieked Aunt Sally. "And you know it! Jeremy didn't do anything wrong. He's practically a draft pick, for God's sakes. Why would he risk all that?"

"Easy," Officer Garrity pleaded to no avail. "Please."

"If anything," Aunt Sally went on, pointing a finger at one of the youths, "Lee roped him into this mess!"

"Gimme a break, Sal," Lee's father rebuffed. "Lee didn't rope anyone. He's not the ring leader-type."

Lee shrank a few inches lower in the chair.

Zoe's mom, Aunt Fran, leaned in, pointing a finger. "That's true. I think we all know who the ringleader is when it comes to trouble."

As if choreographed, everyone turned to look in Truman's direction. He didn't move, Lee observed, as they clocked their collective gaze at him. The only sign was the tight clenching of his jaw.

"Truman is not a troublemaker," barked Uncle Bill, reflexively clamping a hand over his son's shoulder. "The lad has a higher IQ than the other three combined."

"He's the only one with a record," Grant Traven shot back. "What was it again? Arson?"

"Those charges were dropped!" snapped Uncle Bill.

From the corridor appeared Officer Phil escorting Zoe back into the chaos of the lobby. The parents pounced on him.

"Well thank you for joining us, Officer," said Aunt Carol with a lethal edge in her tone. "Can we please clear this up?"

"I'm sorry for the wait, folks," Officer Phil said. "It's been a long night."

"Can we take our son home now?" pleaded Aunt Sally, clutching Jeremy's shoulders tight. "Is this nightmare over?"

As the parents sprang on the senior officer, Lee ejected himself from his chair and zeroed in on Zoe, left adrift in the swarm. He took her hand.

"Zee? You okay?"

Her face was drawn and blanked. Eyes puffy and red with no trace of green in the hazel. She seemed oblivious to the racket all around her.

"Zoe," Lee said. "What happened?"

Her mother barged in and dragged her daughter away. "Don't talk to him," Aunt Fran hissed, strafing Lee with a withering look. "He's caused enough trouble as it is."

Lee fumed but said nothing. How had he been tagged as the bad one here? As Zoe was pulled out of reach, he looked across the room at Truman. His spindly cousin with the cast watched the chaos with an expression of impatient contempt.

Aunt Sally all but clawed at the police officer. "Can I take my son home now? I think he's been through enough already."

"Yes," declared Officer Phil, surrendering to the collective enmity in the room. He turned to Zoe's mother. "Fran, you can take your daughter home, too. And keep them there for now until I can clear this up."

"Done," spat Aunt Fran, marching Zoe to the door.

"I mean that," warned Officer Phil. "If I see any of them on the street I am going to haul them back in here."

Lee felt his arm tugged as his father yanked him toward the door. His path was blocked by Officer Phil, who clamped a hand over Lee's shoulder. "Except for Lee," he said to Grant Traven. "Lee and I still need to talk. Same with Truman."

Uncle Bill jerked his head up in disbelief. "What? What do you want with him?"

"I still need to question Lee and Truman," said the officer. "Zoe and Jeremy can go."

His father sputtered in confused anger at the man in uniform. "What're you talking about? We're done here, aren't we? These stupid charges are dropped, right?"

"No, the charges stand," said the police officer.

Every parent in the room flinched.

"Phil, what the hell? Drop the stupid charges."

The police officer shrugged. "That's not my call. You'll have to speak to the person pressing the charges."

Aunt Fran was apoplectic. "And who is that?"

"Talk to the King," replied Officer Phil. "Now I need everyone to go home. I'll drive the boys home when I'm done. Go on."

Fran dropped a few choice words to the policeman before shooing her daughter away. Truman let out a long sigh and flopped into a chair. Lee remained caught in the police officer's grip. His stomach dropped watching Zoe and Jeremy exit the police station.

"Lee, take a seat," said Officer Phil. "Truman, you're up first. Let's go."

Letting out another exasperated groan, Truman rose and slunk after the officer. Passing Lee on the way, he gave his cousin a smug wink. *I got this.*

The parking lot of the Carthage police station was crowded with the vehicles of the Traven clan who had come to rescue, or possibly murder, their wayward children. The eastern sky was beginning to purple with bruised clouds at the approach of dawn.

Leaning against his dusty Ford pickup, the King bit off the point of a cigar and coolly struck a match, puffing on the stogie until it was lit. Turning to look back at the police station, he smiled. Even from across the parking lot he could hear the chaos of shrill voices within.

A whirl of smoke billowed around his face and he looked up at the glow of the dawning sky, pleased as punch.

"Gonna be a beautiful day," he said and climbed into the cab.

The hard-backed chairs of the lobby were cheap and uncomfortable. The fixed armrests made it impossible to stretch out and Lee wondered if this was by design. The local constabulary probably didn't want anyone loitering too long in the station's lobby.

His stomach churned with a dry ache. How long had it been since he'd eaten? Tilting up to the big clock behind the reception desk, he realized it was mid-morning. Truman had been held for questioning for almost three hours. What the hell was taking so long? What was he saying to friendly Officer Phil? Was he spilling his guts, confessing the whole thing? Sending them all down the river in the process? Or maybe cousin Truman was just betraying him, throwing him under the bus like so much trash.

He thought back to the weird blasted look on Zoe's face when she emerged from questioning. Same as Jeremy's. Had it been just exhaustion from being interrogated after such a long, weirdly exhilarating night? Or had something happened in that room to make both Zoe and Jeremy return with guilt stitched across their faces?

Lee retrieved his phone and tapped the screen and frowned when it did not light up. Holding down the start button to reboot the stupid thing achieved no results. He had hoped that the stupid thing had dried out after its plunge into the black water of the old well but this was not the case. Remembering the incident triggered an immediate recall of the leering skull rolling up from the muddy depths. Along with the visual was a tactile memory of the slime-coated bone on his fingertips and he felt an abrupt need to scrub his hands with soap. Or maybe vinegar.

Christ. How much trouble were they in? They had found a body in the well and dug up a child's grave. If anyone found out what they had done, the four of them would be considered monsters.

Twisting this way and that in the uncomfortable chair, Lee finally gave up and stretched out on the floor. He closed his eyes. Maybe this was all just a nightmare that would be forgotten when he awoke at home in his own bed.

An earthquake shook him awake; a hand on his shoulder, shaking him relentlessly. He blinked stupidly up at the police officer.

"Hey buddy," said Officer Garrity. He had kind eyes. "I got you some breakfast. Or lunch. Whatever."

A styrofoam carton was held before him, emitting a heady aroma. Lee sat up as Officer Garrity placed the carton in his lap.

Lee rubbed a knuckle into his eye. "What time is it?"

"Half past one," stated Officer Garrity.

"One in the morning?"

"One P.M." The officer nodded at the carton in Lee's lap. "Eat up."

Lee's hands were awkward and clumsy as he opened the lid to find a sandwich stuffed with a fried egg and strips of bacon. Biting into it, he grunted something meaningless like a caveman. Each mouthful cleared his head by small degrees and his hands lost some of their clumsiness. He was thirsty.

A noise tore his hazy attention from the meal on his lap. Officer Phil emerged, escorting Truman back through the lobby. Like the others before him, Truman wore a hangdog expression as he shuffled past. He did not look at Lee.

"Sean, take Truman home," Officer Phil said to his subordinate. Then he turned to Lee. "Three down, one to go."

Lee sat there with a mouthful of half-chewed sandwich bulging his cheek. There was something unsettling in the officer's words. Ducks in a row, waiting to be shot down. Officer Garrity opened the front door and Truman shuffled out of the police station into the bright sunshine.

Rubbing the back of his neck, Officer Phil yawned. "I gotta make some phone calls, Lee. Sit tight for a spell."

Lee slumped forward, his spirit shattering. "Can't we do this tomorrow? I've been here all night."

"Finish your breakfast. I won't be but a minute."

The officer left the room. Lee set the sandwich aside on the next chair, the food settling queasily in his stomach. He closed his eyes and tried not to think about the loot they had hastily buried out in the field. Or the fact that his three cousins were free while he languished inside the police station. Or his supposed uncle with the sideburns and slicked hair.

22

Pumping iron - Hey hey, my my - A jigsaw puzzle - The stricken patriarch - First cup out of the pot - A giddy sense of vertigo - Lying to authorities - Remanded

JEREMY STOOD IN the garage, looking out the smudged window of the roll-up door. After spending the night in the chilly field and then detained at the police station, he had slept till late afternoon. Breakfast had consisted of a protein shake and an extra large helping of parental condemnation. His father had bellowed and fumed, shaking his fist at him. Did he have any idea what he was throwing away, he had said, by getting into trouble? His whole future was at stake. And over what?

Jeremy sat quietly and took his punishment. Having little interest in Lee's stupid scheme in the first place, he was honestly remorseful for his actions, his contrition genuine.

As always, his mother interceded like a referee between the two and calmed her husband's fury. Although his father assured him that he would be punished for being so bloody stupid, he had yet to state any specific disciplinary action. The whole thing had blown over when Jeremy's mother fried up a mess of hash and eggs for both of them.

As per the police officer's demand, he remained at home the rest of the day. By late afternoon, Jeremy was bored and listless and went to the garage to work out. Ten minutes on the bench press but he was too distracted to concentrate. He tried playing Fallout but the game he had obsessed over now seemed silly and pointless. Noticing the mud caked on the ATV, he began wiping it down only to give up on that also. After a while he stood at the roll-up door, looking out the window at the empty street.

As much as he hated to admit it, his father was right. A mistake like this one could cost him his position on the team. The coach was a strict law-and-order man who never missed church. He wouldn't abide this kind of stink on his team, no matter how talented the player was.

Lee and his stupid ideas. How had he been talked into such a ridiculous plan? He wanted to wring Lee's scrawny neck. And there was still the matter of the sin they had committed. Desecrating a grave? What the hell were they thinking? Recalling the sight of that small skeleton made his stomach turn and when he contemplated the idea of the police finding the open grave, Jeremy covered his mouth, afraid he was going to vomit. Had any of the others told the cops about it? How much worse would it be if Officer Phil found out that he had lied to him?

Lee and his stupid ideas.

And yet the plan had worked. They had found the bags of outlaw gold, just like the legend said. And just as quick they had been forced to rebury it in the middle of an empty field. It was still out there, lying under a foot of loose soil.

Stepping away from the window he turned the music up and went back to the bench press. Gripping the bar, he lowered the weight to his chest and began pumping as the harsh crunk of guitar filled the room and a wobbly voice crooned.

Hey, hey. My, my.

Rock and roll can never die.

———————————◆◆◆◆◆———————————

Across town, on a quiet street of shady elm trees and split-level ranch homes, Zoe was thinking the same thing. Two satchels of gold coins hidden under dirt in an open field. Anyone could come along and take it. The question was, would any of them try? The four of them had vowed not to but that had been before being hauled off to the police station. All because of their creepy uncle who thought he was the reincarnated king of rock and roll.

The puzzle piece slipped from her father's fingers and fell to the floor. She bent to pick it up.

"Don't lose any pieces," she said to him. "Or we'll never finish this thing."

Like the others, Zoe had endured a round of rage and guilt from her mother when they had gotten home. Her father had only mumbled a few unintelligible words. And then it was over.

Confined to the house, Zoe had retreated to the dining room

where a thousand piece puzzle lay spread over the large table. The image on the puzzle was a Norman Rockwell painting that held two mirror images of a family in a car out for the day. In the top image, the family appeared happy and eager to get to their destination. The bottom image was its opposite, showing the family returning spent and drained from their outing. It was hokey in that idealized nostalgia of Rockwell paintings but there was something to it that appealed to Zoe. Probably the dog, hanging its head out the window.

Her mother was the puzzle nut in the family, happily taking on these enormous jigsaws with thousands of pieces but since the stroke, her father had taken to sitting at the dining room table silently scanning the array of pieces. His compromised speech and motor skills had made him withdrawn and gloomy, preferring the solitude of puzzles to the outside world.

She placed the dropped piece into his hand and he attempted to slot it into the puzzle. The trembling was so acute that he scattered a finished section of the jigsaw puzzle. His face darkened at the betrayal of his own muscles. His jaw tightened as he struggled to force words out his mouth.

"I...am...sorry."

"Don't be," she said, reassembling the pieces. "It's just a puzzle."

"No," he wheezed. The exertion of speaking even a few words was draining him. "About...school."

It caught her off guard. He was referring to their abruptly compromised income because of his stroke and the clipping of her wings in secondary education. It was clear just by his eyes how much he loathed being so feeble, so needy.

"Don't be," she repeated, patting his hand but looking away quickly, fearing the tears might erupt any moment.

Her mother entered the room with a handful of pills and some water, allowing Zoe time to compose herself. She watched in shared mortification as her mother placed each pill on her father's tongue and lifted the straw to his lips to wash it down. Like a child, incapable of the most basic of functions.

Excusing herself, she went upstairs and closed the bathroom door behind her. Splashing cold water over her face, she stood looking into her reflection in the mirror. Her father's condition was worse than she thought. Back at university, among her friends and the new life she had made for herself there, it had been easy to fool herself that her father would get better and that life would return to normal. That he would be back to work and she would return to university in the fall. Seeing his hand scatter the puzzle pieces had brought the truth smashing down on her. Her return to school was forfeit, her new life a mirage that vanished into nothing like heat shimmers on a summer road.

She padded out of the bathroom to her own room and pushed the curtain in the window aside. She was exhausted, running on no sleep from the night before and the torment of the police station. And rumbling beneath the concern over her father and the loss of her new life was the unrelenting pull of a fortune buried in an untended field.

Her phone buzzed. Slipping it from her pocket, she looked at the caller name on the screen and frowned. What did he want?

<hr />

The Carthage Police station had one interview room that, given the town's modest population, was rarely used. The last time it had been employed for that purpose was three years ago when Derek Keene drunkenly plowed his Jeep Wrangler through the plate glass window of Sharon Marsten's flower shop on Main Street. Since that incident, the unused interview room had become a storage area that was now too crowded with boxes to accommodate its purpose. So Officer Phil Carson improvised, using the office kitchen as his interview room.

The industrial strength coffee maker was gurgling with a fresh pot as Lee was told to sit down at the long table. The sugar dispenser had been pushed to the far end to provide a clear area of the table, alongside a matching set of salt and pepper shakers in the shape of Jersey cows.

Officer Phil poured a cup from the pot and took a seat across from the young Traven kid.

"So, Lee," he said, blowing the steam from his cup. "What were you digging for out there on the farm?"

The aroma of the java wafted across the table. "That smells good," Lee said. "Can I have a cup?"

"In a minute. Let's get through some of these questions first." Officer Phil sipped his coffee and almost sighed. "Mmm. I love that first cup out of the pot, don't you? Sharp and strong like that?"

Lee licked his lips. He was still chilled from the wet clothes and night air and he wanted nothing more than to wrap his cold hands around a hot mug.

Officer Phil opened a notebook. "We know you were looking for something out there," he said, tracing a finger down the bullet points on the page. "But I have three different answers as to what it is. So what was it, Lee? Arrowheads or a Viking grave?"

Lee looked down at the table. Three summers ago, Truman had once dared him to walk the handrail of the span bridge over the river. It was less than three inches wide. If he fell to one side, he would land on the sidewalk but if he fell the other way, it was a straight plunge down forty feet to the rocky creek bank. He had that same giddy sense of terror now but he had no idea which was the safe side to fall.

"Who cracked?" he asked, looking up the officer. "It was Jeremy, wasn't it?"

"That's not really important right now," the officer replied.

"I should have known. Jeremy just folds to any hint of authority."

"Jeremy's a decent kid. He knows right from wrong." Officer Phil set the cup down on the table. "I know this whole thing was your idea. It was you who wanted to break into the barn and steal your grandfather's property. And that you conned your cousins into helping you."

Lee felt his stomach flip. "They blamed me?"

Officer Phil, despite his amiable smile, possessed a hard stare that bored into Lee's and never looked away. The man didn't seem to blink. "Are you telling me this wasn't your idea? Then whose was it? Jeremy? Zoe?"

Lee tried to match the hardness of that stare but he failed and looked away. The best he could manage was to keep his mouth shut.

"Just tell me what you were looking for," the officer said, "and this will all go a lot easier."

"We weren't looking for anything." Without any idea of what his cousins had told the officer, Lee wasn't sure how wise it was to go with the original story they had decided on. But at this point, what did he have to lose? "We were just hanging out, one last time on the farm before it's sold off."

The uniformed man looked disappointed. "You sure you want to stick with that story?"

"Yup."

"Have it your way." Officer Phil closed the notebook. "You are formally charged with two counts of breaking and entering and four counts of theft under a thousand dollars."

The coffee maker had finally stopped gurgling. Lee sat there with a stupid look on his dirty face, realizing he had fallen on the wrong side of the rail. Straight down to a hard splat.

The officer went on. "Now, as a favor to your dad, I'm going to remand you into his custody for now. You'll be notified of your court date."

Lee's voice cracked when he tried to speak, one last cut of shame. "Am I free to go?"

Officer Phil nodded but when Lee rose from the chair, he added a parting comment. "Lee? Stay away from the farm. If I catch you out there again, I'll have no choice but to detain you."

23

**Ghosts in the church bell - Reconnaissance - Out of the blue
and into the black - A brief history of escape - Peeping Tom -
Ride along - The empty skate park**

SAINT PAUL'S ANGLICAN Church stood at the intersection of
Main and Willow, the very heart of town. Its bell tower rose three
hundred feet into the air and, if one was to scale the rickety
staircase within it, its portal windows offered a commanding view
of the whole township of Shackleton.

Truman sat in the north window, butt on the casement and
one leg dangling down over the sheer drop to the shrubbery
below. Bored, he had stuffed his backpack with a set of high
powered binoculars, two tall cans of beer, a bag of pretzels and a
half-empty pack of cigarettes. Thus outfitted, he had slipped out
of the house and down four blocks to the footing of Saint Paul's
church. Scaling the buttress wall and breaking into the tower was
a snap. The climb up the winding staircase inside the bell tower

was treacherous and thrilling the way it shuddered and creaked under each step, threatening to collapse under him at any moment. The bell itself was magnificent up close, a behemoth of greenish bell bronze that had been decommissioned decades ago. And, to the romantically minded, it was also haunted. On his fifth or sixth climb into the bell tower, Truman had stuck his head up inside the great bell and, listening closely, he had heard voices whispering all around him. He knew that it was just a weird reverberation of local sound caught inside the metal bell but it sounded eerie and unearthly to his ears. He preferred to think of the lost souls inside the church, drawn to their own funeral service, becoming trapped inside the bell with no way to escape. Thus they whispered and moaned, entombed within the dead ringer.

Scaling the rattletrap steps this night, he didn't bother craning his head into the bell to listen to the dead. His agenda precluded any such silliness. Perched in the narrow window like some lesser Quasimodo, he unzipped the backpack and removed the high-powered binoculars and scanned the town around him. From the vantage of the tower, he could see the homes of his fellow conspirators. Angling the binoculars to River Street he could peer through the garage windows and see Jeremy lifting weights. He also knew the tired playlist that his cousin favored and Truman could tell that the hockey player was pumping to Neil Young's masterpiece. His foot tapped along unconsciously to the buzzy backbeat.

Out of the blue and into the black...

You pay for this, and they give you that.

Scanning the lens west across town, he drew a bead on Tilson Avenue but the window of Lee's room was dark. Either his cousin was sitting in his room with the lights off or he wasn't home. Did he sneak out? Annoyed, Truman swung the binoculars northeast to Victoria Street where he clocked Zoe standing in the window of her bedroom. Gazing at the outside world, she seemed lost. Two out of three wasn't bad, but he remained unsettled at finding Lee's room dark. Did he slip out? Was he that ballsy?

Like his three compatriots, Truman had also been confined to quarters but he'd been sneaking out of the house since he was eleven years old. On his birthday last year, he had vowed to Jeremy that he was going to get his own place in town. No more living with the parental droids. Who could endure them anymore? By October he had secured a small bachelor above the Yarn Barn on Main Street and, for two glorious months, had lived like a king. When Christmas rolled around, he was broke and unable to pay the rent. His parents refused to subsidize his expenses when he had a perfectly good room at home and so, with hangdog shame, he moved back home, the party over. That October-November run had been the best two months of his life and he wanted more, but the harsh truth was that minimum wage pay at Sandusky's Auto Glass Repair was insufficient to underwrite such a venture. He could either eat or pay rent, but not both.

His old man never missed an opportunity to remind Truman of his failure, pointing out the ways he had recklessly blown through his money and failed to budget accordingly. His mother wasn't so harsh but her sympathy was colored by a treacly condescension that made his molars ache. Since then, he had begun scraping together every penny he could manage and kept a bag packed in his closet, ready to go at a moment's notice. He had vowed to his friends that one day, when the opportunity came, he would simply vanish.

And now this further humiliation. When Officer Friendly imposed the lockdown, his father had doubled-down, ordering him to stay home for the next three days. He was to go to work and return straightaway. Sneaking out of his bedroom window with the binoculars stuffed into the backpack had been simple enough but it was just one more sharp point of humiliation for him. Twenty-years-old and still sneaking out his parent's house. Pathetic.

Perched in the casement window of the bell tower, he leaned forward and spat, watching the glob of spittle fall to the junipers below. He adjusted the lens of the binoculars and scanned Lee's house again but his cousin's window was still dark. What was that little shit up to?

What were the odds that Lee was halfway to the farm right now, intent on digging up what they had collectively buried there? Lee had had a boner for this whole treasure hunt right from the start. If any of them was likely to break the vow and run off with the horde of gold, it was Lee.

Sweeping the spyglass back across town, he clocked Jeremy still lifting weights before checking in on Zoe. She had moved out of the window and was folded into the armchair in her room, scrolling through her phone.

He retrieved his own phone and tapped a number on the contact screen. Observing her through the binoculars, he watched his cousin check the caller I.D. before answering the call.

"What do you want, Truman?" she said, coolly.

"We need to talk."

"I'm busy."

He smiled at that. "No, you're not."

As if stung, she whipped her head around to the open window. "You're such a creep. Are you in the bell tower again?"

"Best seat in the house." He frowned watching her draw the curtain.

"One of these days you're gonna fall and break your neck."

"That would make it easier, wouldn't it?" he said. "Make it a three-way split, instead of four."

A pause, then she said: "We shouldn't even be talking right now."

"We need to talk. Now."

"I can't leave now," she said.

Stymied by the drawn curtain, he lowered the binoculars to his lap. "Yes, you can."

———————— ◆◆◆◆◆ ————————

Lee squinted his eyes as he finally stepped out of the Carthage Police Station, anticipating the full bore of the bright sun. After thirteen hours inside the gloomy confines of the police building, he fully expected to blinded by the pure light but he wasn't. The sun was arcing low over the western edge of town, the day drawing to a close.

"Jesus," he said, moving stiffly down the pathway to the rear parking lot. "What time is it?"

There had been no clocks inside the kitchen, no digital display from a microwave and his phone remained dead in his back pocket. He had no way to track the hours wasted inside the makeshift interrogation room.

"Gone seven," said Officer Phil. He nodded to the patrol car parked near the fence. "Climb in."

When the officer opened the back door, Lee stopped. "Do I have to ride in the back?"

"Standard policy." Officer Phil watched the young man's hangdog face pull even lower to the ground. "What the hell. We'll bend the rules this time. Just don't tell anyone."

Small mercies. He would have sooner walked home than be seen riding in the back of the cop car. The passenger seat was cramped by the laptop bolted to the panel. Officer Phil swiveled it out of the way, allowing his passenger a little more elbow room. Lee looked at the customized gear and control panels within the driver's reach. It looked more like the cockpit of an airplane than a car.

They cruised down Main Street. Lee watched the barber shop and the payday loan place pass by the window, ducking a little when he saw a few people on the street.

"See this?" Officer Phil held up a small remote control,

hovering his thumb over the various buttons. "This is for the cherry lights on top. This is for the siren. Guess what this button does?"

"Ejector seat?"

The officer laughed. "No. If I hit this one, it will turn all the traffic lights green for me."

Carthage had four traffic lights. Five, if you counted the one out on Highway Nine. "Cool. You never get caught in traffic."

"It only works if the cherries are flashing." They turned onto Tilson Avenue, past the realtor's office, and then Officer Phil glanced at him. "You graduated this year, didn't you?"

"Yeah."

"That's great," said the officer. "You off to college in the fall?"

"I didn't get accepted."

The officer was trying to chit-chat but Lee felt too numb to talk. He watched the houses drift by. The evil Fermen brothers were playing on the sidewalk. They held a cinderblock and were taking turns dropping it on something at their feet. When the police car rolled past, Lee saw that it was a box turtle. Officer Phil bopped his horn and the boys ran off.

Lee picked at his blistered callouses. Then he turned to the officer. "Say, you and Uncle Elvis are friends, huh?"

"We go back a long time. I wouldn't say we're best buds or anything. But yeah, we're friends."

"Did he ever go to jail?"

Officer Phil scowled at the question. "Who told you that?"

Lee shrugged. "I heard he killed somebody. In a bar fight."

"Well, first off, that's his personal business and I do not truck with gossip." Officer Phil tapped a button on the console, then added: "He may have been incarcerated a long time ago, but it wasn't for manslaughter."

"Then what did he go away for?"

The officer scowled again. "Like I said, I don't like gossip."

They drove on, passing the new skate park behind the old department store. It consisted of one bowl with three drop-ins, a few rails, and one half-pipe. Constructed two decades ago, it was still referred to as the 'new skatepark'. No one went there now, not even to smoke weed or kill time. Lee was surprised to see it occupied now; two people standing near the rail but it was too dark to identify them. He did, however, snap a double-take when he spotted the Nissan Pathfinder parked there.

Didn't Truman's parents drive a black Nissan? Was that him? With Jeremy? Lee pivoted to look out the rear window but the skate park was out of range.

The abrupt shift in demeanor was not lost on the police officer. "You okay, Lee?"

"Fine." He settled back into the seat, mind racing. A ball of ice began forming in his guts. Up ahead, the streets were mostly empty. One car approached, then passed them. A Volvo station wagon. Aunt Fran's car? Headed in the direction of the skate park? The Volvo had zipped past too quickly to see who was behind the wheel.

"I'm fine," he said again.

24

Tea in a time of crisis - Aping contrition - Enraged mater, defeated pater - Paying the piper - Horror films - The Pathfinder

"HOW COULD YOU be so stupid?"

The question echoed around the kitchen for, what seemed to Lee, like the tenth time. His mother bellowing it at him, fists shaking. Did she expect a different answer each time she said it? Or any reply other than the stony silence he offered up?

The kettle had boiled but was left forgotten as his mother paced across the scuffed floor. When faced with a crisis, Diane Traven's first response was to make tea.

"Do you have any idea at all about how bad this looks for us?" she railed. "Or how it reflects on the business? Did you think about that at all? No, of course not. Why would you? Your father is livid. Just livid!"

Lee remained still, wondering what had happened to his

father. They had returned home twenty minutes ago, both he and his mom ejecting from the car. His dad stayed behind, slumped behind the wheel as the engine ticked and knocked as it cooled. Was he still out there, sitting in the car or had he simply driven away, too disgusted to even discuss it?

Stupidly, Lee spoke up, realizing too late that it was too early to utter anything. "Mom, it's not that bad."

"Not that bad? Are you kidding me?" Her anger kindled back to life just as it was tapering to an ember. "I've never seen your father so angry. God knows what he's going to do to you."

The side door, two steps down from the kitchen, swung open and the patriarch in question ambled through, tossing his keys into the ceramic bowl on the counter. The bowl was a misshapen lump of fired clay that Lee had made when he was nine-years-old. Somehow it had survived the jangle of keys and loose coins after all this time. Scrawled into the bottom of the glazed ceramic were the words 'Happy Mother's Day'.

Lee steeled himself for another round of hollering. His father flopped into a kitchen chair and smeared the back of his hand over his brow but he didn't speak a word. A minute passed and then another, his father just staring out the sliding glass doors that led to the patio. Impatient with her husband's silence, Diane took her tea and marched from the room.

Lee waited, stymied by his father's unusual silence. He clearly wasn't following the usual script when it came to punishing his only child's latest screw-up.

Bracing for the worst, he tried to undercut it by speaking first.

"I know you're mad, but—"

"I'm not mad," his father said. "Not anymore. I'm just...I'm just tired."

Lee kept quiet, unsure where this was going.

"You're not a kid anymore," his father went on. "You can't get away with stupid choices now. There are consequences, real ones."

"Dad, I can explain—"

"Yeah, you will," his father replied. He rose from the chair. "But not to me. We're not going to contest the charges. You're going to man up and take what's coming to you."

"You can't be serious."

Halfway to the door, his father turned and looked back at him. "It's very simple, son. I could stand here and yell at you for hours for what you did, but we both know it won't make a damn bit of difference. So, maybe the judge can get through to you."

With that, he turned and left the room, leaving his son alone to consider his future.

Had he imagined the black Pathfinder and Zoe's station wagon or were the others meeting up behind his back? Lee knew he wasn't thinking clearly, his brains fried from not having slept in the last 24 hours.

Still.

He stood on the front porch trying to decide what to do. Call

Zoe. She's probably at home, curled up on the sofa watching a bad horror movie. Where other people's comfort movie was something funny or feel-good, for Zoe it was horror flicks. And the gorier the better. He'd never understood it himself. Sci-fi movies were his thing, even superhero flicks, but not horror. They all seemed dumb to him, but Zoe ate the stuff up. So that's where she would be right now, hand in a bowl of popcorn as she watched someone's head get taken off with a chainsaw. Call her and find out.

But what if she's not? What if the three of them are on their way to the farm now?

Fuck it.

Borrowing the car was out of the question unless he wanted to sneak it out. But that would require putting the car into neutral and pushing it silently out of the driveway before starting it up. Too risky. He'd have to take the bike.

Cutting through back alleys and empty lots, he was downtown within minutes, rolling up within spitting distance of the skate park. The black Pathfinder sat parked at the curb but of the Volvo, there was no sign. Had he been mistaken about the whole thing? Was the lack of sleep playing havoc with his eyesight?

Then, voices. There, at the bottom of the concrete pool with its ramps and curved walls, stood his three cousins. Huddled close and talking low, their voices warped by the concrete bowl around them.

It felt like a hard boot to the guts, but the sting was shortlived as it bloomed into anger, hot and vindictive. Lee spat onto the pavement and looked down at the Pathfinder'. Clean and polished with barely a trace of road dust. Even the tires were clean. Lee reached into his back pocket, grateful he had remembered the jack-knife.

25

Conspirators assembled - The weak link - A boxed ear - Cornered into a confessional - The crippled Pathfinder - Nowhere to run - Backed into a gender role - Shrill knuckles on glass

"NO," SHE SAID. "We have to wait."

Truman looked disgusted. "We can't wait. Lee's gonna be at the cop shop all night. We're outta time."

Zoe stepped away, her Nikes scuffing the concrete floor of the bowl. Truman was putting the pressure on and Jeremy said little, as usual. Nothing ever changes, she thought. This same dynamic had played out when they were kids and here it was, happening all over again. The only thing different was the point of disagreement.

"We have to do it now," Truman implored. "Before Uncle Creepy finds it."

Jeremy nodded. "He's right. We might already be too late."

She turned back to face them. "What about the promise we made?"

"That was before we got hauled into the cop shop," Truman snapped. "Forget the promise, we gotta adapt to the new situation."

Feeling her resolve weakening, she was about to lob one more counter-point when a screeching noise preempted her.

Bicycle brakes, Lee rolling his bike down the ramp, brakes squealing from misaligned calipers. He dismounted and let the bike clatter to the ground.

"Which one of you broke?" he demanded. The question appeared to be rhetorical as Lee marched on the eldest of the four cousins. "You. You fucked me over."

"Hold on—"

Lee sprang. Caught off-guard, Truman tumbled flat on his back with his cousin on his chest. A hard fist to his chin, another sharp against his ear before he could buck the little shit off.

"Get off, psycho!" Jeremy barked, yanking Lee up and tossing him aside like a sack of dirt.

Truman scrambled to his feet, one hand palmed over his boxed ear. "What the fuck!" he screamed at his cousin.

Lee was panting hard, eyes a little crazed. "You ratted me out. You told the cop I was some ringleader in this."

"It was your idea, fucknuts!"

Lee jabbed a finger at him. "You screwed me over, knowing I'd be stuck at the cop shop so you could sneak back for the loot while I'm up shit creek. Did I get that right or did I miss a step?"

Jeremy stepped in Lee's path, blocking him. "You screwed yourself," he said.

Lee redirected his venom at the hockey player. "Don't you ever get tired of being his lapdog, Jay? He says jump and you ask how high?"

Jeremy's face darkened. He lumbered forward until Lee backed away.

Truman kept his palm clamped over his stinging ear. "I didn't rat you out, you idiot."

"Bullshit. You tried to cut me out, you lying sack of shit."

"Like you haven't been scheming to cut me out?" Truman looked at his palm, expecting to see blood. There wasn't any. "I wasn't the one who cracked."

"Then who did?"

"Ask your cousin."

Jeremy. He should have known. But Jeremy sneered at him with contempt. "Don't look at me," he said.

More lies. Had to be. But Jeremy had never been a good liar. The tops of his ears went red when he lied. And right now, there was no blush to them. But if he didn't do it then...

"Zoe?"

Her eyes darted around, alighting on everything but him.

Truman piped up instead. "Do you want to tell him," he said, "or should I?"

Lee blinked, mouth hanging open. "It was you?"

Cornered, Zoe stammered. "I had to."

Abrupt and harsh, like a hammer against piano keys. Denial

took over as Lee muttered to himself. No, no, no...

"He wanted to pin it on me," she said. "The cop said he would make it worse if I lied to him."

Lee tried to catch his breath. "What did you tell him?"

"The truth. Or most of it." She smeared her forearm over her brow. The night had turned humid.

"Jesus, Zoe. Why?"

Zoe stiffened, grasping for something to say, for a way to make him understand.

Truman leaned close and hissed in Lee's ear. "She sold you down the river, bro."

Another gut-punch. Lee staggered. "How could you?"

"Because it was the truth. You broke into the barn and took the stuff, Lee. I wasn't going to let that cop pin it on me." Something flared in her eyes, desperation or anger. Possibly both. "I am not getting stuck here. Not for this, not now."

Truman hooked his cast-clad arm around his neck and whispered into his ear. "Face facts, cuz. She's a lying bitch."

Even as little kids, Truman knew how to wind all of them up. How to egg Lee on into doing something stupid, how to prod Jeremy into a rage or needle Zoe to tears. Little had changed. Lee was still easy to wind up. Pulling him close, Truman whispered awful things into Lee's ear until Lee's face darkened.

Something snapped and Lee lashed out like a rattlesnake, bashing Truman's face as hard and as fast as he could manage. A full-on Hulk rampage, like flipping a switch.

Jeremy simply frowned, annoyed at being forced into the role of referee again. He let them go at it for a moment, scrabbling and kicking on the floor of the concrete pool before stepping in. A hard kick to Lee's stomach and another boot to Truman's skinny ribs and the two were separated, moaning in pain.

Lee was first on his feet, winded but still rabid. He spun around, looking for Zoe.

She was gone, vanished in the scrum. Another trait from childhood. She would often walk away when the boys turned violent.

"You're a fucking dead man," Truman spat, eyes bright with murder.

Lee was already scrabbling up out of the pool, dragging his bike over the edge. He didn't look back as he pedaled away but he heard Truman calling after him.

"Run, faggot! Pedal back to the farm, you fucking loser!"

Hitting the main drag, Lee skidded to a stop. The streets were empty, no sign of the Volvo anywhere.

———— ✦•◆•✦ ————

Hauling themselves out of the pool, the two cousins walked out of the skate park toward the alley.

"The hell did you kick me for?" Truman wanted to know, his good hand over his ribs.

"Because you deserved it," Jeremy said.

Truman dabbed at his swollen lip, annoyed to see blood on his fingertips. More annoyed that Lee had landed a few good shots.

He looked west, the direction that Lee had fled. "Does that dumbass think he's gonna race us back to the farm?"

Jeremy marched on ahead, uninterested in his cousin's griping. Rounding the corner of the building, he stopped cold.

"Son of a bitch."

They had left the Pathfinder parked behind the Quicky-Mart convenience where the street lighting was poor. It was difficult to see what was wrong with the vehicle. Truman moved closer until he could see the tires were flat. All of them deflated, the valve stems removed.

"I'm gonna murder that little shit," Truman said.

———————— ◆◆◆◆ ————————

She drove aimlessly for the first while, turning left onto Arsenal Street and then back to the main drag, over the train tracks and back again but the inevitable truth is that within the confines of every small town, there is really nowhere to run to.

Not that she had any destination in mind. Just the need to keep moving as if stopping meant getting sucked down into a quagmire that would swallow her whole.

Watching the yellow lines of the road blip-blip under her headlights, she indulged in a fantasy of simply driving away. All the way back to Kingston, back to university and a life blessed with no connections to her old self. But the gas gauge was at a quarter tank and her pockets held no more than a few dollars.

The Volvo drifted back to her street as if possessed of an inner homing instinct. She rolled up the driveway, killed the engine and sat in the darkened car. Only the porch light was still on. Everyone was asleep, all was well here.

What options did she have now? Go back to find the others and play peacemaker again, like she had so many times in the past? As the only female among them, the role of mediator had always fallen to her when the boys turned on one another and, like a dupe, she had played her part to make everyone get along. Screw that. Those days were over and if the three of them wanted to thump each other like apes, so be it.

The other course of action was to drive back to the farm and find the buried loot before they got to it. The funny thing was that none of them would expect her to do that, no matter what bullshit Truman had hinted at. They assumed that she would play fair, that she wouldn't be duplicitous, simply because she was the girl among them. How typical, how predictable of them.

All of that loot was just sitting there, buried under a foot of loose soil. All she had to do was go get it. And, cursing her own nature and predisposition, she wouldn't even take it all. A quarter of the shares would be enough to help her parents and provide another year of university. Maybe two.

The harsh rap of knuckles on glass rattled her out of her thoughts. Her mother's voice cut like fingernails on a chalkboard.

"Honey, what are you doing? You know you're not supposed to leave the house."

Zoe kept her gaze on the house, deaf to the figure banging on the driver's side window.

"Come inside now," her mother insisted, becoming shrill. How she hated to be ignored. "Of all the stupid stunts to pull after that nasty business this morning."

The fantasy of driving away resurfaced. The keys were still dangling in the ignition. Starting it up, she reversed back onto the street, leaving her mother stranded in the driveway with a confused look on her face.

26

High lonesome road - A hole in the ground - All-terrain Apaches - The return of the King - Graceland - Under the horse blanket - .44 cartridges - Shake hands with the Devil

THE LONESOME ROAD was silent and desolate save for the lone cyclist pushing hard along its gravelly path. A quarter moon hung high and cool in the sky, casting a pale blue wash over the landscape. When the headlights of an approaching vehicle lit the road behind him, Lee went down the embankment to the ditch and hid until it rumbled past. Peppered with a scattershot of pebbles from the passing tires, he popped up to identify the vehicle and breathed easier when he saw that it was neither the crippled Pathfinder nor Aunt Fran's practical station wagon.

By the time he got to the farm his legs were burning and his shirt clung to his back. A single light was on at the house, a dusty bulb over the backdoor that forced Lee to stop and listen before moving on. Was someone here or had the porch light been carelessly left on? No other lights appeared, no movement anywhere. The only sound was the droning of bullfrogs from the creek and the eternal chirping of crickets. He moved on.

Past the shadowy ruin of the barn and out onto the plain, he left his bike on the edge of the field and proceeded on foot toward his best guess to where they had hastily buried the trove. Traipsing through the weeds this way and that, a flutter of panic lit his belly when he saw no hint of the marker they had left behind. An X of neon construction orange spraypainted onto the ground. Was the paint invisible in the dark? Was it gone completely, blown away or obscured by a strong wind? Cursing, he retraced his steps, back and forth across the field while keeping a lid on his erupting panic. Then he stumbled, his foot plunging into a gopher hole. A sharp snap of pain to his knee as he landed all wrong.

The orange paint became visible in the moonlight, sprayed cold onto the dirt. This was no gopher hole he had stepped into. A small excavated pit no more than two feet deep and nothing more. The bags of gold were gone.

They had beaten him to it.

The pain in his knee was forgotten, replaced by the humiliation of tears. They fell hot and shameful and would not stop no matter how much he scolded himself. Low on his knees in the dirt, he let gave up and let himself blubber like a toddler.

Which one had done it? All three had plenty of time to sneak back here while he was stuck at the police station. Truman was the obvious culprit. Or had all three of them conspired against him, retrieving the loot while he was being questioned and then acting innocent when confronted about it?

The temperature was dropping and his sweat-damp clothes would chill him to the core if he didn't get out of this stupid hole but he could not muster the will to get up, to move on. What was the point?

A dull buzzing sound rumbled in the night air and the sound of it chilled him more than the dew. A dot of light bounced out in the rising fog as it came roaring over the plain. Lee ducked but realized how pointless that was. He was a sitting duck in the middle of this empty field and the approaching ATV was rumbling right for him. He imagined his own face, stupid and blank, in the headlights of the all-terrain-vehicle.

He bolted for the barn. Backlit by the headlights, he knew it was impossible to outrun the quad-runner but if he could make it to the perimeter, maybe he could dive through the brush to hide. The roar of the engine overtook him and something hard crashed across his back, sending him hurtling to the dirt. Rolling to his knees, he saw two riders on the ATV. The passenger on the back was wielding a hockey stick, howling some kind of war cry like an Apache warrior of yore. The faces of the riders were obscured under the helmets but Lee knew who it was. The dynamic duo of backstabbing, double-crossing, motherfucking cousins.

The ATV circled back. He rabbited south, then east but each time the vehicle cut him off, forcing him back. They were toying with him, circling like a shark around prey, when the Suzuki suddenly jerked sideways against an unseen dip in the terrain and the back rider was thrown. Lee sprinted for the barn, thundering blind out of the field but the uneven earth sent him sprawling to the ground. Scrabbling up, he was blinded by the harsh headlights. The thrown rider marched on him, wielding the stick like a war club.

Another set of headlights cut open the night, angled on the two riders. The rumble of a different engine was heard as a battered pickup truck came out of the fog, gunning for the helmeted duo. They dove out of the way and the truck thundered hard against the idling ATV. It tipped onto its side and rolled over like a carcass, wheels in the air.

Lee panted, dumbstruck at the spectacle.

The passenger door popped open, the dome light illuminating the driver. Uncle Elvis barked at him. "Get in!"

Lee flung himself inside and the truck jerked in reverse and then plunged forward. Gravel spewed from the wheels as Elvis swerved onto the road. Lee twisted around to look through the rear window. He only caught a glimpse of the two riders circling their overturned vehicle before the whole farm disappeared around a copse of poplar trees.

He clenched the handrest on the door but his hands felt numb. Everything felt numb, his nerves fried, brains scrambled from the panic.

Uncle Elvis glanced into the rearview mirror and shook his head in disdain. "Those goddamn ATVs," he said. "Menace to all creation those things."

———————— ◆•●•◆ ————————

The rusty pickup rattled through the darkness on backcountry pathways that left Lee unsure of where they were until the truck swung onto a paved road that he recognized as Highway 9.

Another mile on this route and then Elvis turned onto a dirt track that cut through a glen of scrub pine and black oak. A ramshackle house rose up in the glare of the headlights. The front yard was turned out with a few rusting appliances and the bulk of an old wood stove. A black Cadillac hovered on cinderblocks, its dark skin dusty with pollen.

The driver swung out of the cab and strode for the clapboard house. Lee closed the passenger door but ventured no further.

"You took it, didn't you?"

The man's boots clomped up the porch steps. "Watch that last step," Elvis said. "It needs mending."

The screen door clapped shut behind him. Lee sighed and followed. A wooden sign hung from the porch rafters. The letters carved into it read: *Welcome to Graceland.*

Stepping across the threshold, Lee cast his eyes over what must have been the parlor at some point but now resembled a bachelor pad gone to seed. Crates of records were stacked five high next to an old hi-fidelity cabinet that glowed with a green warmth. A nude in black velvet was framed over the fireplace. Leering from the mantelpiece were two taxidermied crows, their black plumage frosted with dust. Book-ended between the stuffed birds lay a double-barreled shotgun.

A light went on in the next room, the sound of a fridge rattling open. Uncle Elvis's voice rang out from the doorway.

"Grab a seat."

Every chair seemed occupied with old Playboys or stacked records. The only available seat was on the sofa but it was tattered and stained and Lee stayed where he stood. When his uncle emerged from the kitchen and leaned against the doorway, Lee blurted out the question burning his mouth dry.

"Where is it?"

The older man twisted the cap off a beer and snapped it across the room where it clattered away amongst the junk. "How about a 'thank you'?"

"Thanks," he said with little sincerity. Then he reiterated his earlier query. "Where is it?"

Elvis nodded at something near the window. "Under that horse blanket."

The dusty turnout blanket was draped over a low table. Lee flung the heavy material back to find the two Wells Fargo sacks. He checked the cords on each and found each cinched tight, their contents undisturbed.

"It's all there," the man declared.

"Where's the pistol?"

"Catch."

Lee turned just as Elvis tossed the enormous six-shooter at him, almost dropping it. It was heavy, the gunmetal cold in his hand.

"I could smell the spent powder on it. You boys let off a few rounds?"

Lee touched the scab on his brow, recalling the wallop he took from the gun's recoil. "There was a box of cartridges with it."

"I'm surprised those old rounds didn't blow up in your hand." Elvis sipped his beer, aiming a finger at the antique pistol in the boy's grip. "I chambered in some new .44 rounds. Should work."

Lee thumbed back the lever and broke the gun at the hinge. Six shiny new cartridges were slotted into the cylinder.

"Now you can rob me at gunpoint," said the king.

Lee snapped the pistol closed. He marveled at the weight of it, the sheer size of the barrel. A canon in his hand. When he looked up, his 'uncle' was smiling oddly. God only knew why.

"All you gotta do is point it," Elvis said, "and say 'hands up'. Just like Jesse James."

It was hot in his grip. The other man leaned against the door, sipping his beer, defenseless. How easy would it be to just blow him away? Time seemed to slow to a molasses crawl. Lee could feel the glassy eyes of the stuffed crows staring at him.

The gun lowered. He knew before he even asked the question. He set the gun down on the table and looked up at the man with the sideburns.

"I guess you win, huh? You're a rich man now."

Uncle Elvis shook his head. "It don't belong to me."

"Then who does it belong to?"

"That is the property of the man who buried it." The grin on the King's face fell away, his eyes dimming. "And if it was up to me, he would crawl up out of the fire and take that damned thing back to Hell with him."

"Jesse James?" Lee asked. "For real?"

"The very same."

It was a trick. Had to be. "There's a fortune in gold there," Lee said. "You telling me you don't want it?"

The other man tilted the beer up, draining it. Then he leveled his gaze on the younger man. "Do you want to know the story behind this?"

"Yeah."

"Don't be flip, son," he cautioned. "Secrets come with a price. This one is no exception."

Something was being bartered here but Lee was too exhausted to figure out what it was. The crows wouldn't stop staring at him.

"Yeah," he said again. "I want to know."

27

Terms of surrender - A history unrecorded in any book - Theodore Rufus Traven - North across the border - An ill-tempered horse and an unlucky boy - A visitor in the night - Promises made and kept - The faithful sentinel

"YOU KNOW ANYTHING about Jesse James?"

Lee shrugged. "He robbed banks and stuff. Fought in the Civil War."

Elvis pulled up a chair, spun it around and sat with his arms propped on the backrest. "He was a diehard Confederate who refused to accept the terms of Appomattox. He kept fighting long after the war was over, targeting the banks and railroads of the Unionists. He was a thief and a murderer. His family were slave-owners. He was also a husband, father and devout churchgoer. Sit."

The threadbare sofa creaked as Lee lowered onto it. The Smith & Wesson remained on the table between them and the dead crows looked on from their perch.

The King resumed his narrative. "Your ancestor, Theodore Rufus Traven, rode with the James-Younger gang as they tore through Missouri, Arkansas, and Kentucky, holding up banks and trains. But old Rufus had a change of heart when he was shot in the neck and left for dead with a posse hot on their tails. Rufus hid in the brush and made peace with his maker. Jesse double-backed after dark and spirited him away to a doctor who mended his wounds. But the close call unsettled Rufus and he told Jesse he was quitting the gang. He didn't want to spend the rest of his days running and dodging bullet fire. He had kin up north across the border and he was headed there, beyond the reach of the Pinkertons who were hunting them. He told Jesse he would be welcome there if circumstances turned against him. Hold up."

Elvis rose and crossed into the kitchen, returning with two bottles of Moosehead. The beer was cold and Lee didn't realize how parched he was until it hit his throat.

"So what happened to Rufus?"

"He headed here, to the protection of his kin who had settled in the area. He buys himself a patch of acreage, marries his third cousin, Mary Alice Stiles, and settles in as an honest farmer. They start a family. The first two are born blue but they keep trying and end up with five boys and three girls. The eldest boy, Albert Walker, is kicked in the head by an ill-tempered horse and dies. It was during the boy's wake when a stranger rode up over the plain, inquiring after a Mister Rufus Traven.

"You can guess who it was. Rufus welcomes his old compatriot, shuffling him away from the curious eyes of his family. Jesse was in a bad way, half-crazed with seeing assassins around every corner and lynch mobs behind every tree. He tells Rufus he wants to quit the life too, just disappear and start over. Repent his ways under an assumed name. And he's got a plan, Jesse does. Saddlebags full of loot he wants Rufus to keep safe for him until he can settle his affairs and collect his family.

"Rufus agrees. He owed James his life and was happy to settle the debt. But they needed somewhere safe to hide all that loot. Somewhere real secret. The wake for the dead son was winding down, the hole in the family graveyard already dug. So Rufus and Jesse hide the money in the boy's casket, along with the insurance policy of the Smith 'n Wesson. Rufus promises to watch over it until his friend returns with his family. Except Jesse James never makes it back.

"James' death is all over the newspapers. Shot in the back by one of his own gang members. But immediately the rumors start, that James faked his own death to slip away and was believed to be living grand somewhere far from Missouri. Some say he's headed for Mexico, others believe he's headed north to cross the border.

"And old Rufus, he's unsure what's truth and what's fable, but he made a promise and, God willing, he's going to keep it. What else could he do? He watches over that horde of loot buried with his eldest son and keeps one eye on the horizon for a rider to appear. When he got older and sensed his time was quickening, Rufus recruited another member of the family to keep watch.

Since then every generation of the Traven family has had a sentinel."

Lee took another pull on the bottle but it was empty. "Sentinel?"

"Guardian," Elvis said. "Keeper of the watch."

"Was Grandpa a sentinel?"

Elvis shook his head. "No. He'd heard rumors about it his whole life and became obsessed with it. Spent twenty years digging holes all over creation looking for the damn thing."

The night air blew in through the sashed window, riffling the faded curtain. The sound of crickets and the hoot of an owl. Lee looked down at the satchels of loot and tugged on one of the ties. He came away with a double eagle, turning the gold coin in the lamplight. The gold was dingy, the grooves caked with grime. He looked at the man across the room. "What are you gonna do with it?"

"Put it back where it belongs."

It sounded ludicrous to Lee. "You're not tempted to keep it? Even a small part of it?"

"Only a fool would keep it."

"Why? You afraid the ghost of Jesse James is gonna come get you?"

"I'd be more leery of the ghost of Albert Walker."

Lee thought back to the small papery bones nested within the moldy casket. He didn't want to dwell on the dead child but found it impossible to flush the image from his mind'. He kept picturing the dead boy out there, exposed to the elements the way they had left him. Desecrated and abandoned. Jesus, he was family, wasn't he?

"I told you before," Elvis said, "the damn thing is bad luck. A horde of gold brings about its own peculiar kind of misery." The King stood and collected the empty beer bottles. "You want anothern?"

"Yeah," Lee said. "Please."

The image of the dead boy held fast in his imagination as the other man left the room. Desperate to shoo it away, Lee conjured up an image of a hot-looking woman. A supermodel or movie star, any woman. Zoe, lying flat on a dock, water beading on her skin.

It was interrupted by the sudden crash of the front door being kicked open.

28

On the perils of four-wheelers - The gun on the table - Viva La Vegas - Pistol-whipped - Through the glass and into the trees - Introductory Psychology - A surprise caller

THERE WERE TWO crashing sounds to be precise; one at the front door and another from the kitchen. Lee ducked, thinking the place was being stormed by a SWAT team until he saw the hockey stick. Jeremy had kicked open the front door, Truman had broken in through the back door. They had effectively cornered the two occupants in the parlor.

Truman looked crazed, eyes bright with rage as he turned on the man with the sideburns. "You fucking crazy old man!"

Elvis stood agape at the way his front door hung off one hinge, the glass shattered on the floor. "You boys can't knock? Jesus Christ, look at my door!"

"Shut up," Truman barked, advancing into the room. "Where is it?"

"There." Jeremy pointed at the low table where the satchels lay exposed. He brandished the stick at them. "Back away from it."

Lee felt ice in his blood. The old pistol lay on the table, the shotgun behind him on the mantelpiece. Was he fast enough to go for either before Jeremy broke his skull? Doubtful. Jay was a triple threat: big and fast and vicious when he wanted to be.

Truman barged past him to the sacks of loot. He lifted the one with the loosened cord, looking down at the tinkling currency. Then he leveled his gaze on Lee. "I shoulda known you'd try to screw us all, cuz," he spat. "You always were a sneaky little shit."

Elvis regarded the intruders with disdain. "Leave it alone, Truman," he said. "It ain't worth it."

"Shut up!" Jeremy raised the stick high, ready to do some serious damage. "You fucking trashed my ATV!"

"I was doing you a favor, son," Elvis said. "Those things are a goddamn menace."

There was a moment, a heartbeat or two, when the others were busy barking and swaggering when Lee saw a chance to grab the pistol but his limbs were rigid. *Do it!* he prodded himself. *No one's watching!* But he hesitated and, as the saying went, all was lost. Truman spun and snatched up the old Schofield .44.

The long barrel came up and drew level with Uncle Elvis' face. Truman's eyes narrowed to slits as he regarded their relation with the slicked hair. "Who the fuck are you, anyway?" he queried. "All our lives, you've been kooky old 'Uncle Elvis', but no one seems to know shit about you. Are you even related to us or is that all bullshit?"

The King nodded at the bore hole pointed at him. "I doubt that antique works, son."

Truman's thumb bent back the hammer until it clicked. "It works just fine. We tested it. That's how dipshit there got his head bloodied. Didn't Lee tell you?"

The night went quiet, the crickets and owls ceasing their racket. Either that or the thrumming pulse in Lee's ears blocked out everything. This wasn't really happening, was it? A bad dream, a bad movie on TV?

Their uncle became very still. Whether it was the steadiness of Truman's hand or the crazed wet look in his eye, Lee couldn't tell but Elvis seemed to cotton to the very real potential of having his face blown apart.

So did Jeremy. Like their uncle, he had assumed Truman was posturing as he so often did. But the expression on Jeremy's mug passed quickly from amusement to concern.

"T," he hissed, "quit screwing around, man."

Truman just grinned. "Viva las Vegas," he laughed. And then he pulled the trigger.

"No!"

Lee winced, expecting to feel the wet spatter of blood and brains spray against him but the spatter never materialized. Truman had bucked the gun up, firing into the ceiling where it rained a little dust. Elvis had ducked, hands up against the blast. When he realized the shot went high, he looked up in time to see the pistol swinging down hard.

The sound it made was a dull smack as the metal rind of the

pistol handle bludgeoned against the older man's head. Uncle Elvis dropped instantly like a puppet with its strings cut. Thudding against the worn-out floorboards, he didn't move.

"What the hell are you doing?" Jeremy sputtered. "We said we weren't gonna hurt anyone."

"Man the fuck up, Jay," spat Truman. "You know what you signed up for. Don't go all pussy on me now."

"Are you fucking crazy?" Lee gasped. The shock had loosened his tongue but he immediately regretted it as the hammer cocked down a second time and the barrel swung level with his eyes. Dead reckoning, with no chance of ducking the shot.

Later, when trying to remember the order of events, Lee would never be able to recall exactly what had occurred. He remembered shards of glass all over him and the hard impact of landing against the porch boards. The gun roared, cracking sharp into the night.

Lee bounded off the porch and bolted into the night, plunging blind into brambles that tore at his face and hands before coming up for air to realize that he was alive.

Another shot from the gun silenced the crickets and he felt a puff of air near his ear as the bullet rippled through the branches around him. He flattened to the earth and crawled away on his belly.

⸻

The hole in the ground gaped like a festering lesion in the earth. Hastily exhumed, the prize hauled away. Zoe dropped to her knees, letting the flashlight clunk to the grit. Making a choice to reclaim her lost future had been difficult enough, the race back to the farm exhilarating and frightening at the same time. Searching through the empty field in the dark had been tortuous and now this, this empty hole in the ground.

They had beaten her to it. One or all of them had tossed aside the promise they'd made and spirited away the treasure they had found. How could they do that to her? She was the one who recognized that something was off about Grandpa's grid-marked map and hunted down the older cartography that revealed the original sprawl of the Traven farm. How sleazy? How fucking ungrateful? How ultimately male.

So. Which of her no good, dipshit cousins had betrayed her? Truman was the obvious candidate; cunning, manipulative and wily as fuck. She had taken Psych 101 that first semester at university, her favorite classes. The lecture hall was filled, almost every student there was female. That didn't surprise her. By late October, the professor began an introductory section on the classification of a psychopath. Every pair of ears perked up, eager for gory insights into Hannibal Lecter and Ted Bundy. At its basic level, there were two distinguishing attributes of the clinical psychopath; a morbid lack of empathy and a skill for manipulation. She, along with everyone else in the class, was pondering the same question after hearing the definition: Does that describe anyone I know?

Truman had a knack for getting into all kinds of trouble but he also had an almost spooky ability to worm his way out of any serious punishment. He could convincingly act contrite, remorseful and repentant to any authority figure, only to laugh at their gullibility later. He had a gift at reading people and telling them exactly what they wanted to hear. Once he had guiled his way out of any serious punishment, he scorned the whole matter and blamed the gullible authority figure for their own stupidity. It had unnerved Zoe on more than a few occasions how easily he could morph to any situation and feel nothing but contempt for anyone who had fallen for his deception.

So Truman was the standout suspect. Jeremy didn't enter the picture unless he was following Truman's lead. Jeremy could be a bully and he was physical, but it was all show. He wasn't cruel and he wasn't deceptive. He had a marshmallow core under all that bluff and she had witnessed it on more than one occasion. Never with the other cousins, just her. He was oddly sensitive but fiercely guarded about revealing that to anyone but her. She could safely cross Jeremy off the list of backstabbers.

And that left Lee. Could he have done that to her? After everything they'd gone through? She had compartmentalized it all, consigning it to a weak phase last summer that she still didn't completely understand. She refused to feel shame over it but chose not dwell on it either. Move on. But Lee operated on the opposite spectrum. He clung to it as some sort of preservation from his circumstances. In its absence, he had elevated it to something more than what it was, something almost spiritual. His salvation but that was unfair and selfish. She was no one's savior except her own.

Pushing herself up, she felt a chill ripple across the back of her neck. The cooling breeze allowed her to focus. Forget the reasons for the betrayal, the only question now was how to get the loot back. Or, at the very least, recover her share of it.

The phone chimed in her pocket. Retrieving it, she wondered which of her cousins was calling. She frowned at the name on the screen. Why was Uncle Elvis calling her? And how did he even know her cell number?

29

Porchlight through the brambles - The marauders flee - Graceland in ruins - A bleeding scalp and a call for help - No names given - A box of shotgun shells - The perils of excessive speed on a dirt road

A CARPET OF DRY pine needles nestled against his cheek as he lay panting on the ground. After a while, he rose and crawled back toward the flicker of light cutting through the trees.

Graceland came into view through the dipping boughs of the pine trees. Shadows passed before the window, moving from the ramshackle house to the ATV in the yard. The two marauders hauled the sacks of treasure onto the rear cage of the vehicle and lashed them with the bungee cords. Pulling the helmet back on, Jeremy climbed on and hit the ignition but nothing happened. The two riders spoke, poking around the vehicle, exchanging words Lee could not hear. Jeremy shoved his cousin away and dropped the pedal into position. He kicked it down over and over before it fired. The engine sputtered unevenly and a greasy black smoke emitted from the pipe. The second rider climbed onto the back and the ATV rumbled away, misfiring like a drunk staggering home.

When the rumble of the engine faded, Lee crawled out of the thicket toward the dingy porch light. Graceland was trashed. The door hung tilted at a wrong angle and broken records lay scattered everywhere. The furniture was overturned, tables swept clear and kicked over. It wasn't enough for the two cousins to bludgeon the older man and take off with the treasure, they felt the need to demolish Graceland in the process.

The floorboards creaked under his steps as he crept inside. Two of the lamps had been smashed, leaving a dark gloom and long shadows stretched over the upended furniture.

Lee whispered into the dark: "Elvis?"

No response. A few more steps into the gloom and the motorcycle boots emerged from behind an ottoman. The older man lay sprawled on his side, as still as stone.

"Shit."

Blood trickled from a deep gash just under the hairline of his Presley pompadour, partly congealed and sticky to the touch.

"Elvis, wake up, man," he hissed, shaking the man's shoulders. He didn't know what to do.

The older man remained unresponsive, the eyes slits of rolled-over white. A sour tang hung in the air and Lee noticed the man's face was smeared with something dark. More of it was puddled on the floor. He had vomited. Wasn't that sign of a concussion?

Scrambling over the trashed floor until he found the telephone, a clunky old rotary dial with a cord. Flipping it upright he jabbed at the plunger until he got a dial tone and then spun the awkward rotary disk.

Five rings before a dispatcher came on the line. "Nine-one-one," said a voice. "What's the nature of your emergency?"

"My uncle's been hurt. He needs an ambulance!"

"What's the nature of his injury?"

"He got knocked in the head. Like really bad. He's passed out and there's blood."

The dispatcher's voice was maddeningly calm. "Is he breathing? How bad is he bleeding?"

"He's breathing. But he puked all over himself. Hurry."

"What's your location, sir?"

Lee stammered as his mind went abruptly blank. He couldn't recall his own address let alone this old shack hidden among the pines outside of town. Panic bubbling up fast, he babbled and spat into the receiver. "Chokecherry Road, just off number nine. I don't know the number. It's the last house near the river."

"Okay," replied the calm voice. "What's your uncle's name?"

"Elvis." Said aloud, it sounded ridiculous.

There was a pause. "Elvis what?"

Another blank ballooned inside Lee's skull. Did he even know Elvis' surname? He wasn't even sure if Elvis was his real name. Was he a Traven or a Gallagher, the clan on his grandmother's side. Frustrated, he chose kinship.

"It's Traven. I think." His eyes had adjusted to the dim lighting and his uncle's face grew sharper. It was gruesomely pale. "Please, hurry. Jesus, what do I do?"

"Stay calm, sir. Can you tell me your name?"

"Huh?"

"Your name? Tell me your name."

What the hell was she talking about? His name wasn't important, he just needed a goddamn ambulance. "Who cares! Just get an ambulance out here before he dies—"

"Sir, I need you to remain calm. This will go much easier if I can address you by name."

He dropped the phone back into its cradle. The bell pealed inside it and he looked down at his uncle.

"Hang on. Help is coming."

He looked at his hands. Sticky with blood. He wiped them on his jeans and scurried to the kitchen, returning with a dirty dishtowel that he clamped over the wound.

What now? He couldn't think straight, too much noise rattling inside his head, but he knew he couldn't be here when the ambulance arrived. Out here in the backcountry, sound carried. He'd hear the ambulance a mile away. He could stay with Elvis until he heard the sirens and then slip out the back. But that meant stumbling through the dark on foot.

He picked up the phone again and punched in another number.

Come on, he thought, listening to it ring and ring. *Pick up!*

"Hello?"

Finally. "Zoe? It's me. Jesus, this is so bad." His words gushed out, tripping this way and that.

"Goodbye—"

"Zoe, wait! Please. Truman went nuts. He bashed up Elvis and took off."

There was a pause. "Where are you?"

"Graceland."

"What?"

"Elvis' house, out by the river." A noise crumpled behind him and he spun around. The shadowy room was still, no raiders coming back to finish him off. "Truman cracked him over the head with the pistol. He's just lying here. I don't know what to do."

"Is he okay?"

"He's breathing. I called an ambulance." He pressed the receiver closer to his ear. There was a rumbling hum on the other end of the line, making it difficult for him to hear her. "Are you at home?"

A pause, more low humming. "Where's Truman now?"

"He took off with Jeremy," Lee said. "They took the money and booked outta here on the ATV."

Another drip of silence. When her voice returned, it was frosty. "You went back for it, didn't you?"

This time he let the pause tick on. "Yeah."

"And now you want me to help you?"

"I didn't know what to do! I panicked. I thought you were all out to screw me over, okay? The treasure was gone when I got there."

"You expect me to believe that?"

"Elvis dug it up."

"So he was after it all along," she said, sighing heavily down the line.

"Yeah. But not how you think."

A low groan issued from the man on the floor, followed by a twitch of his leg. His eyes remained white slits.

"I don't what to do," Lee said. "This is so fucked up."

"Is he still bleeding?"

Lee lifted the cloth to check the wound. "I think it's stopped."

"Keep pressure on it until the ambulance gets there."

Reapplying the cloth, he said: "I can't be here when the ambulance comes."

"Just stay calm," she cautioned. "Where did Truman go?"

An idea cut through the panic. Rifling the King's pockets, he came away with the keys to the pickup truck. Agency. A choice drifted up through the clusterfuck around him. Anger came hot on its heels. "I'm gonna kill that son of a bitch."

"Stay where you are," Zoe said. "I'm on my way."

"No. Meet me on the way, on Highway Nine. I'm taking Elvis' truck."

"Wait, Lee—"

The phone clattered into its cradle. He wiped his hands on his jeans again but the sticky blood was still there, clotted under the fingernails. With the keys rattling in hand, he darted for the door but then stopped. The shotgun. He snatched it from the mantel and broke it open at the hinge. Twin bores, both empty. He searched the mantel and the shelf, knocking books and knick-knacks to the floor until he found a box of shells. Remington brand, twelve gauge with red hulls. They dropped and rolled across the floor as he slotted two into the barrels and snapped the firearm closed. Four more shells were stuffed into his pockets before he marched out of Graceland.

The old Ford wouldn't turn over and Lee cursed and bashed his fist against the dash and then he heard the siren in the distance, getting louder. He took a breath to calm his nerves, gave the gas pedal one quick tap and tried the key. It grumbled to life and he reversed recklessly down the path to the road. The engine complained as he pushed it harder and the spool of empty road lit up in the headlights before him, twisting left and then right. Taking one hairpin turn, he realized too late that he was going too fast.

The rear wheels skidded along the loose gravel like it was ice and the ass end of the pickup swung out, hit the shoulder and the whole thing tipped into the ditch with the driver tumbling loose inside the cab.

30

Dying four-stroke - A dry creek bed - All I ever learned from love was how to shoot somebody who outdrew you - The dead Ford - Light through fractured glass - Claiming birthright - A solitary traveler on the high plains - The burden of gold

PROGRESS THROUGH THE backcountry was slow, hampered by the sputtering and popping of the engine. The all-terrain-vehicle rumbled down an embankment, through a dry wash and the driver revved it hard to take the incline of the opposite bank. The laboring four-stroke roared in protest and stalled, died. The ATV rolled backward, thudded over a rock, and tilted to one side.

Truman landed hard on the stony creek bed, the breath knocked from his lungs. His heels bit into the pebbly dirt as his leg flattened and he gasped for oxygen.

Jeremy fared a little better, rolling as he hit the ground to mitigate the impact. Accustomed to hard knocks, he caterwauled to his feet and shrugged off the pain. Too angry to register anything much beyond the destruction of his beloved King Quad. It had already taken a hell of a knock from the old man's truck and now he had rolled it.

"Son of a bitch," he grunted, pushing the quad-runner upright. The front fender was split, the rear cargo cage bent out of whack. The precious cargo, he noted, was still lashed securely to the rack. Climbing back aboard, he adjusted the manual choke and booted down the kickstart but the engine trickled without firing. Two, three, six tries but it refused to catch.

Truman staggered up the grassy incline to his cousin. His helmet was off and his sweat-dampened hair was plastered across his brow. "Come on! Get us out of here."

Jeremy clawed the helmet off and bowed his head. "It's dead."

"Jay, quit fucking around," Truman barked. "Fix the goddamn thing and get us out of here."

Jeremy dismounted, hurling the helmet away in disgust. "You shouldn't have done that."

"Not now, numbnuts. We can't stay here."

"This is crazy," Jeremy seethed. "This is absolutely fucking crazy."

Gauging his cousin's temperature, Truman softened his tone. "Jay, don't lose it on me. We need to book."

"You tried to shoot Lee, for fuck's sakes! We might have killed Elvis." Pounding back and forth, Jeremy wiped a hand across his eyes as if trying to flush some image away. "What the hell is wrong with you?"

Truman shifted to a conciliatory mode, needing to talk his cousin down from the ledge. "Jay, take a breath. You don't think clearly when you get red. Just chill out and think about where we are."

"Fuck you!" Jay shrieked, his cheeks flushed red. "We gotta go back and check on the old man. What if he's dying? We gotta call an ambulance. Maybe the cops—"

Truman lashed out, snatching his cousin by the collar. "It's too late for that. We can't go back. We have to go all the way now."

The taller cousin wouldn't stop shaking his head no matter how hard the other shook him. "No..."

Truman pushed him back to the crippled four-runner. "We don't have a choice now. If we go back, we are fucked. Now fix the fucking ATV and get us out of here!"

"Then we're fucked!"

Jeremy shoved Truman away and reached over the gas tank to pluck the keys from the ignition. He didn't see the antique revolver in Truman's hand, nor did he see it swing high and come down whistling. He crumpled under the impact and folded in half and rolled down the bank to the sandy grit of the creek bed. A low, guttural moan hissed out of him and then he went silent.

Truman ripped the keys from his hand. "In for a penny, in for a pound," he said.

Clambering back onto the ATV, he slotted the key in and kicked at the pedal. And kicked and kicked.

The glow of the headlights looked all wrong, crackled and multiplied like the compound sight of an insect. Lee blinked at it stupidly before he understood that the windshield was cracked in a spiderweb of fractured safety glass. He tried to sit up but everything hurt at the same time and he laid still, breathing through the spasms.

Crumpled in a heap against the passenger door with the steering wheel above him, he struggled to get his bearings. The truck was on its side in the ditch. He recalled the hairpin turn, the feel of the rear wheels fishtailing but he could not remember the crash itself.

Dummy.

Unfolding his legs and shifting into an upright position took forever and the exertion left him shaky and lightheaded. He looked up. The only way out was the driver's side door above him but the thought of climbing up and pushing the door open left him feeling nauseous. He went still to reserve his strength and keep his stomach down.

A light flared up over the cracked windshield, followed by the low rumble of an approaching car. It rolled up close and shut down, the headlights dimming. The sound of a door opening and closing, footfalls on gravel. The cop or the ambulance. Either way, he was screwed.

"Hey," he called out. "Who's there?"

A shadow fell over the fractured glass, then bent low. The face was obscured in the honeycomb of broken windshield but the voice was unmistakable.

"Lee? Are you all right?"

"Zoe?"

The cavalry had arrived. Her palm appeared on the glass. "Are you hurt?"

"Everything kinda hurts." He looked down at himself but it was dark and he couldn't see if anything was bleeding or broken. Something rigid was right up against his ribs and he pushed it away. The shotgun, jammed across the cab. Was that what he had hit his head on?

"Can you climb out?"

He glanced up at the door above him. It may as well have been on the moon. "I don't think so."

"Cover your face."

"What?"

"I'm going to kick the windshield in," she said. "So cover your face."

"Wait—"

Tiny shards rained over him, the racket of breaking glass amplified inside the cab of the pickup. A second kick sent more pieces over the hands covering his face, into his hair. When he opened his eyes, a dark patch of open sky gaped through the windshield. Not big enough to crawl through but he felt the cool breeze rush in. Then her face framed in broken glass.

Her eyes scanned him up and down but saw no blood. "Is anything broken?"

"I don't think so." He shifted again, trying to get on his knees in the cramped space. "It just hurts like a son of a bitch."

"Which way did they go?"

"What?"

"Cover your face again," she said.

He did as he was told, expecting another shower of glass and more noise but all he heard was a crunching sound. Peaking through his fingers, he saw her arm stretch inside the cab and slip the shotgun out.

"What the hell are you doing?"

"They went north, didn't they? Straight across the wind farm toward town."

This wasn't happening. "Zoe, stop. Help me out of here."

Zoe broke the shotgun to reveal two loads in the barrels. She looked at him again. "Are there more shells?"

Four of them, to be precise. All crammed in his pockets. It was a wonder one of them didn't go off, blasting buckshot into his ass. "No," he lied.

"Sit still," she said. "Help is on the way."

Zoe rose to her feet. Through the gap in the broken windshield, all he could see were her sneakers and the barrel of the twelve-gauge. The skin on her left knee was scraped raw.

"Zoe, stop. You can't go after them."

"Yes, I can."

He pushed at the fractured windshield but the glass cut into his palms. "You can't just leave me here! For fuck's sakes, Zoe. You can't betray me like this!"

She crouched down again, her face zooming into the crackled

space. "You betrayed me first, Lee. You got greedy." She looked back at the road and seemed to wince at something before she turned back to him. "We always swore we'd never turn out like our parents, but you? You're worse."

She rose. He panicked. "Zoe, stop. You can't—"

"The hell I can't!" Her teeth gnashed. "I'm going to get what's mine. And you and Jeremy and Truman can all go to Hell."

"Truman's crazy! He'll kill you."

He kept calling after her but she was already across the road where the Volvo was parked. She didn't look back.

⊰•◆•⊱

A solitary figure moved across the plain, trudging through knee-high strands of barley. A flashlight in hand but it was still dark and when his footing slipped, he pitched into the weeds. His burden flopped to the ground with a heavy thud.

The two satchels of gold had been lashed together by the cords and slung over his shoulder but the weight of it was immense and the cords bit into his flesh.

Wheezing, Truman looked up at the distance before him and tried to gauge his progress. The ATV had been abandoned, leaving him no choice but to ferry the loot on foot. How much further to town? Everything in the distance was dark as pitch and all around him were the strange sounds of nocturnal things that skulked and slithered in the night. With the compass on his phone to gauge direction, he could only approximate the correct course. Through the marsh and onto the bottomland near the wind farm with its massive white silos turning slowly in the night. From there he would ford the creek to the wooded area that hid the old graveyard. Then on to the Traven farm and the road back to town.

He massaged his shoulder where the straps had cut into his flesh and then he hoisted his burden up. The heavy satchels pressed against his chest and back, his balance tipped sly under the weight. He moved forward, stumbling over the uneven ground. The marshland was blessedly dry from the lack of rainfall and he made it across without losing a shoe in the muck. Back on solid ground, he rested for a moment to catch his breath.

His spirits lifted when he looked up and saw the white towers and rotary blades of the wind silos before him, like ghosts turning slowly in the night.

31

Dying headlamps - One wretched traveler meets another - Another vehicle left for dead - An albatross of tarnished currency - The bones of Albert Walker - Clicking the hammers - Cornered by a cousin - 44 calibers tucked in a belt - A shot in the dark

THE PICKUP LAY lay on its side in the reeds of the ditch like some dead brute put out of its misery. Maneuvering in the cramped space of the cab, Lee kicked at the fractured windshield until the safety glass was large enough to crawl through. The effort of climbing out left his forearms scraped raw and his stomach reeling. When he crawled out of the muck of the ditch to the road, the headlights of the pickup dimmed to black as the battery gave up the ghost.

The road ahead was a watery blue under the fingernail of moon and he limped along slowly like some haggard wretch chased away from his tribe to die on the wastelands. His face grimaced with each step and his sneakers scuffed the loose stones of the road ahead.

When a light materialized on the road before him, he stopped and scrambled down into the ditch again to hide. There was no sound and the light did not advance and when Lee realized that it was not an approaching vehicle, he clambered back up to the road.

A lone figure appeared on the desolate road, another wretched traveler stumbling along with a flashlight in hand. A drunk walking home? Like a mirror image, Lee wondered if this lonely wanderer had ditched their vehicle too. Staggering and reeling across the gravel, it looked more like a zombie from a bad movie than a drunk. As it lurched closer, Lee froze when he recognized the blue-lit face.

"Jay?"

Jeremy didn't respond. He just staggered forward like the walking dead, eyes dazed and far away. Blood had trickled down the left side of his face, more of it clotted in his hair.

Lee gripped his cousin by the arm. "Jeremy, stop. What happened?"

The other boy blinked as if waking, his eyes rotating to Lee. He kept walking. "Get away from me."

Lee staggered alongside him. "Jay, stop. You're bleeding. Let help me help you—"

He reached for his arm again but a hard shove sent him skittering backward.

"I don't want your help," Jeremy grumbled. "I want you to get the hell away from me."

The gravel crunched as he continued his momentum. The rose of light from the flashlight swung across the road before him.

"Jay, tell me what happened? Where's Truman?"

Jeremy stopped and swept the flashlight full bore into his cousin's face. "Is that all you fucking care about?"

Exposed in the glare, Lee turned away from the light.

Jeremy spat and walked away. "Stay the hell away from me. I don't even know you anymore."

When the ATV lit up bright in the throw of her flashlight, Zoe stopped and swept the light beam over the terrain. Trees and bullrushes, the twisting path of the dry creek, but no sign of her cousins. Swinging the light back to the vehicle, she noted the cracked fender and bent bars of the cargo rack. She pressed a hand against the shell and found the engine still warm. The keys were still in the ignition. The rear cargo rack empty.

Her cousins must have gone on foot from here, carrying the loot. The question now was which direction did they go?

She climbed up the bank, her shoes slipping on the loose dirt until she crested the rise and looked out over the darkened plain. The open field of barley dipped and rippled under the throw of the flashlight until a swath of flattened weeds marred its pristine expanse. A tell-tale pathway trampled through the field.

The barley stretched out like a sea across the plain. In the distance she could just make out the turbine blades of the wind silos to the north and to the west was a rise of trees that held within it the graveyard they had desecrated. The trampled path of weeds cut right for it.

She went down on one knee, laying the flashlight and shotgun aside, then she tightened and retied the laces of her shoes. If at some point, she needed to make a run for it, it wouldn't help to lose a shoe on the way. Straightening back up, she gathered her tools and followed the trampled path into the sea of barley.

———————————◆◆◆◆◆————————————

The burden grew heavier, as burdens do, with each stumbling footfall and the cord cut into his shoulder so deep it left welts on his flesh. He took to dragging the sacks of gold after him but he soon dropped to his knees from the effort. Peeling off his shirt, he folded the damp garment into a rectangle and draped it over the raw welts on his flesh. The padding reduced the pain as he slipped the bags back over his shoulder and pushed on.

Reeling past the birch trees, he followed the rough path into the hidden graveyard and stumbled through the headstones. His course had remained true, cutting the shortest path through the fields and into the graveyard. At the other end of the copse was the creek and beyond that, the farm. There was no way he could ferry the burden all the way back to town but the Traven farm was big and sprawling. Plenty of places to hide the loot for the time being. He needed to go home, get the air pig from the garage and go back to the Pathfinder downtown. With the tires re-inflated, he would come back for the sacks of gold.

Halfway through the cemetery, he went down again as the weight bested him. Massaging the mangled muscle meat of his shoulder, he saw a dark gap in the earth to his left. He didn't want to look at it but could not keep his eyes from the yawning hole. He crawled to the edge of the open grave and angled his flashlight down. The open casket lay at the bottom, its withered occupant exposed to the cooling night air.

He looked away. The flashlight splashed across the headstone of the boy's grave. Died 1880, aged nine. What had he died from? Typhus or consumption? A beating from his father?

Click. A sound, sharp and out of place.

"Kind of apropos, huh?"

Whipping around he saw Zoe upright between the headstones. Her hands clutched a double-barreled shotgun, her thumb still on the hammer she'd locked into place. Narrowing his eyes, he flushed the surprise from his face. If there was one thing he hated, it was losing his cool. Gave the other person too much power.

"Hey, cuz," he said, straining hard to sound casual. "Where'd you get the boom stick?"

Her flashlight swept over the graveyard, eyes darting around for something but never straying too far from her cousin with the cast on his arm.

"Where's Jeremy?"

Truman took his time to turn his head and spit. Buying time to size up the situation. "You got any water on you?"

"Where's Jay?"

Truman wagged his chin at some indeterminate spot behind her. "He's around somewhere. Could be anywhere."

It did the trick. Zoe glanced quickly behind her. There was nothing there, nothing but nightfall and forgotten gravestones. Her eyes kept darting about, flinching at every lonely owl hoot, pupils dilating to pinpoint a cousin that wasn't there.

"I guess you come for it, too, huh?" He nodded at the two stained sacks on the ground.

"Stop talking." She hollered out at the darkness. "Jeremy! Come out here!"

"And here I thought you were better than all this, Zee," he said. An odd smile tilted his features at some joke that only he was privy to. "You know, you used to fool me with that act of yours."

"Shut up."

"The whole holier-than-thou routine," he went on. "I fell for it ever since we were kids. Dunno why though. Cuz you're a girl maybe? Or maybe it was the way you'd roll your eyes at us like you couldn't believe you were related to such retards."

Zoe waved the barrel again. "Move back. Away from the sacks."

He didn't move. Instead, he laughed. "You should have gone into acting, Zee. You've a real knack for bullshitting people into what you want them to see. The good girl, the motivated student, the cousin with ambition and goals. Oscar-worthy performance, you ask me."

"Truman," she warned, "shut up. And move away."

It was working and he smiled at that. She was rattled and

startled at every sound, expecting to get ambushed by Jeremy.

"Look at you now," he sneered, his tone a poisonous mix of contempt and superiority. "The good girl holding a gun to her own kin."

The double-barreled gun shook in her hands, quaking from the rising temperature in her glowering eyes. Which is what he wanted. Like a magician with a card trick (which he also was adept at), she was focused on his words and not on his hands. She didn't notice him reaching behind for the antique six-shooter tucked into his belt.

"Christ, Zoe," he growled, "you're worse than Lee."

--------- ◀•◦◆◦•▶ ---------

Out on the moonlit plain, Lee staggered on, following the path trampled by the others before him. Back at the dry creek bed, he had stumbled across the ATV and simply followed the trail. He didn't like where it was leading, back to the stand of trees and the old graveyard nestled behind it.

His mouth was dry and he wanted water but he had none. He trekked on, staggering over the uneven ground. He stopped when he heard the boom, crackling sharp through the night air. The report of a gun.

And then another. Louder this time, booming like thunder.

And he was running, pitching crazily through the stalks as he bolted for the poplar trees.

32

Bang, bang! - The smell of gunpowder - Hard knuckles and bruised flesh - Sixgun in a trembling hand - Mutant offspring - Bleeding out - A denial - Tumbled into an early grave

TWO SHOTS. The sharp crack of the Schofield and the louder boom of the shotgun. Lee tried not to imagine the worst as he crashed through the brambles to the cemetery. Two lights twinkled in the darkness, casting a hazy outline to the tilting headstones. The smell of gunsmoke ripe in the air. Of his cousins, he saw no sign.

Scuttling between the graves, he hissed her name but no reply came. A blur of motion in the darkness of his peripheral vision and he crawled toward it and peered around a stone. No Zoe, no Truman. Just the open grave they had left behind.

The snap of a twig led him to another stone, another cautious peek and there she was. Curled into a tight ball with her hair trailing through the grass.

"Zoe!" he whispered, coming up behind her. Gripping her shoulders, shaking her to rouse her.

She rolled over, wiping a hand over her mouth. There was something wrong with her left eye. Helping her to sit up, he turned her face to the light. Her eye was swollen and purpled, her lip split.

"Did he do this to you?"

He looked her over, checking for any other wound, but she pushed him away. She seemed lost and unaware of her surroundings.

"I heard gunfire," he said.

She sat blinking, trying to focus. "I missed."

"Where is he?"

"Behind you," she whispered.

Truman sat perched on a headstone like some kind of gargoyle, the big pistol in his hand. He smiled at his cousin. "Yonder comes the hero," he said.

Lee felt his pulse tick up and up, enraged by the bloated smugness on his cousin's face.

"I'm gonna kill you."

Truman brought the pistol to bear but the long barrel shook, the hand unsteady. "Bring it on, sporto. I can still aim, despite the damage."

The light cast from the flashlights was poor at best. What Lee took to be a smirk was revealed to be a grimace. The white teeth were clamped in pain. Truman's left arm hung limp at his side. Blood trickled past his elbow and onto the dirty cast.

"She didn't miss," Lee said.

"That's the advantage of a shotgun," Truman said through clenched teeth. "Any idiot can hit the side of a barn with buckshot." His face contorted again, trying hard to twist the grimace into a grin. "Don't matter. I win."

At the base of the headstone lay the sacks of gold coins. The rough canvas was spotted with the blood dripping from Truman's fingertips.

"You know," he went on, "I could never figure out what the deal was with you two. Always whispering and sneaking around. Acting like you're better than everyone else. Smirking like you got some big secret. Then I figured it out. It's obvious, really. You're fucking her, aren't you?"

Oxygen became scarce. Zoe kept her head down. Lee felt his knees go soft.

"Truman, put the gun down."

The pistol waved about recklessly in the shaky hand, the barrel bobbing at Lee and now Zoe and back again. "That's sick, bro," Truman sneered. "You can't get a girl so you stick it to your cousin?"

Lee's eyes darted over the graves around them, the trees beyond, searching for an answer that wasn't there. "It's not like that."

"Oh? Then what's it like?" Truman tilted forward, almost falling from his perch. "Wait, let me guess. It's true love."

"You wouldn't under—"

"Shut up!" Zoe shrieked, cutting him off. She was on her feet now.

"Look who's awake." Truman looked at her, searching out her eyes. "What's the deal, Zoe? You telling me you two freaks aren't bumping uglies? Huh? Answer me!"

Lee held up a hand. "Leave her alone."

"You two are sick." Truman spat into the weeds, underscoring his point. Then he waved the pistol at them. "Back up."

They did as they were told, withdrawing but mindful of the open pit behind them. Truman slid off the headstone, gritting his teeth against the pain.

Scrambling for something, anything, to defuse the situation, Lee said: "Truman, you're bleeding. You need help."

The gunman glanced down at his bloodied arm. His face softened, the pistol becoming heavy in his hand.

"He's right," she added. "You're gonna bleed out if you don't get help."

Truman wavered. Then he snapped out of it, shaking the cobwebs from his head. The gun came up again, leveling at their faces. "Get in the grave," he said.

Zoe's mouth hung open. "What?"

"Get in the fucking grave where you belong!"

Lee wobbled again, his head dizzy. This wasn't happening. "Truman, stop. This is crazy."

The .44 shook in Truman's hand, aiming now at her, then him. "What the fuck is wrong with you two?"

"I told you. It's not like that."

"What were you gonna do?" Truman seethed. "Run away and

have a bunch of retard kids?"

Lee felt tears rising up. He choked them back. "Put the fucking gun down. Please."

Truman moved in, bringing the barrel of the big gun a foot from his cousin's nose. His eyes alight with some feverish hatred, he nodded at the grave again.

"Get in the hole. With her, you sick fuck."

What happened next was unclear, a chaotic blur of noise and violence. Lee thought he was about to die when a banshee wail ripped up the silence and something slammed into the gunman, into his wounded left arm. Truman let out a shriek, folding under the agony. Lee caught no more than a glimpse of Zoe body-checking Truman before lunging for the abandoned shotgun in the grass.

The rest slipped out of sight as Lee careened backward, hands clawing, into the open grave.

33

Sheol - Your dead will live, their bodies will rise - Like a dog - Entreaties in the darkness - Spaghetti western, Mexican standoff - Flayed against a headstone - '68 Come back special - Shovels in the darkness - Are you lonesome tonight?

AN ABRUPT THUD when he hit bottom, a sound like dry sticks snapping underneath him. To his horror, Lee realized it was the cracking of bones breaking under the impact. The papery skeleton of one Albert Walker Traven, aged nine. Panic compounded upon revulsion as he scrambled to get out of the moldy coffin. The shadows were not deep enough at the bottom of the grave to spare him a glimpse of the small skull. It lay partially caved in, the lower jaw splintered. He clawed at the bare earthen wall but the dirt slurred through his fingers like sand, finding no purchase.

The sound of gunfire knocked his revulsion aside but it was too abrupt to distinguish between the report of the revolver or the twelve gauge.

If it was the shotgun, then Zoe had blasted the second barrel.

She would now be out of ammunition. His hand patted his pockets, digging out the shells he had stuffed in them. Three shells, the fourth one must have fallen out somewhere along the way. Didn't matter now. Zoe was defenseless.

If it was the Smith and Wesson that had gone off, then Zoe was probably dead.

Truman's voice bellowed in the night above him, cursing Zoe to Hell, vowing to shoot her down. It was followed by the pounding of feet racing through the weeds. Then silence.

Lee flattened against the dirt wall to make himself invisible to any eyes above. His heels crunched down on the bones again, snapping their dry tinder under his shoes but he refused to look down. His heart was clanging hard but he narrowed his focus down to the single gunshot and Truman's vows of revenge. Whichever one had pulled the trigger, both were still alive. Zoe was running for her life while he was trapped in this ghastly pit.

Do something. Before that psycho kills her.

At five-eight, his vertical had always been shit but he sprang up for the surface, hands clawing and digging at the lip of the grave until one leg swept up and he rolled out. He scurried for cover behind a headstone.

Crack. Gunfire ripped across the graveyard again but from which direction, Lee couldn't tell. Then he heard his cousin's voice bellow up out of the night air.

"Give it up, Zoe! You're out of ammo and we both know it. Step out into the open and we'll talk. No guns."

Stillness came the reply. Even the frogs ceased their croaking as if cocking a collective ear for her answer. Nothing.

Pressed against the sandstone flat of a grave, Lee craned his neck to peer through the cemetery. The glow from the discarded flashlights cast a hazy relief against the tilting headstones. A blur of motion flitted by. Truman stalked through the cemetery, the big gun in his fist, sweeping all of creation for any movement.

Clapping a hand over his mouth, he watched Truman storm this way and that before marching back to the open grave. Lowering the barrel, he fired one round into the pit without stopping to aim. Assuming he had shot the refugee hidden there, the gunman seethed at finding the grave empty.

"Zoe!" Lee hissed into the night. "Where are you?"

Again, nothing. Had she fled the cemetery or was she flat on the ground, bleeding out in the grass?

"Lee?" Truman's voice cut into the night. "Come out, bro! I ain't gonna hurt you."

Low on his belly, Lee scurried to the shelter of another stone, keeping his eyes peeled for any sign of Zoe.

Truman kept hollering, entreating both to parlay. "This is crazy. Zoe! Lee! Come out. Let's put down the guns and talk. There's plenty of gold here for everyone."

The words tugged at something inside Lee. A desperate wish to believe those very words, a childish hope to end this crazy hunt through the graveyard and go back to how things used to be.

Don't listen.

Keep moving.

Find her.

He crept on, scuttling like some clumsy gekko to another stone. He hissed her name into the dark but no reply was heard. Maybe Zoe had done the smart thing after all and simply cut for the trees.

Truman kept calling. "Come out! I swear to God, I'll put the gun aside and we'll divvy up the loot. Just like we said we would. We'll bring Jeremy his share, too. Come on, guys! We're blood, for Christ's sakes!"

Lee covered his ears with his hands to block out the words and then the pistol fired, nearly taking his head off. A piece of headstone broke off and tumbled onto him. He scurried away.

He listened to Truman's footfalls stomping through the tombstones, the sound coming from all four cardinal points of the compass. Everywhere and nowhere at the same time. Any moment now he expected to be shot down, in the back, crawling on his belly like a fucking coward. Another blast of the pistol sang, another headstone chipped.

He scrambled on, face in the dirt. Any thought of finding Zoe vanished and there was just the naked instinct to not die.

Truman's voice again. One word.

"Gotcha!"

Lee looked up, expecting to see the gun barrel aimed at his face. What he saw was only the night sky.

"Game over, bitch," he heard Truman growl, not far.

He eased out from behind the tombstone. Truman stood five paces away but his back was turned. The gun aimed at Zoe, cowering on the ground where she had been uncovered. The shotgun was still in her hands, useless without a round in it.

The cylinder in the old revolver clicked and turned as Truman thumbed back the hammer. He steadied his aim.

Lee shrieked something unintelligible and sprang at Truman before fear froze his limbs again. Truman whirled around and the gun went off and Lee flopped to the weeds like a dead crow. His right hand was on fire and when he raised it up, he saw the raw stump where his index finger used to be. A bloody nub of exposed bone and gun-blacked tissue.

He whimpered like a dog. Truman leered at him in triumph. Neither of them saw Zoe coming but Truman felt it, the butt of the shotgun against his ribs as she swung for the fences. It slipped from her grasp upon impact, clattering to the ground.

The pistol went off again, the aim ruined from the wallop to Truman's ribs. Murder, pure and bright, glistened in his bloodshot eyes as he swiveled the weapon on her and pulled the trigger.

Click.

The shotgun lay in the clover. An eternity played out before Lee pulled his head out of the pain and snatched it up. Blood smeared the grip as he dug for the shells in his pocket. One fell to the ground as he broke the barrel and his hand quaked trying to slot the second shell into the bore.

Truman was already reloading. With the pistol broken and the barrel clamped under his armpit, he fumbled one cartridge and then two into the cylinder and clapped the gun closed and aimed. He fired once but the report was drowned out by the blast of the shotgun.

Smoke ribboned in the air and the smell of powder was sour. Lee remained on his knees. Truman lay sprawled against a headstone, flayed by full-bore buckshot at close range.

Zoe remained frozen, lock-jawed in disbelief as the smoke dispersed around her.

A low mewling noise issued from Truman's shredded lips and his heel kicked into the dirt. The rest of him just leaked blood. The Schofield was still in his grip, the barrel in the dirt.

Lee's grip was slipping, the pain in his hand like fire. He broke the gun again, found the lost shell in the clover and loaded it. He heard Zoe scream at him but his ears were ringing too loud to make out what it was. Later, he would come to understand that she was telling him to stop but in the mute moment he snapped the gun closed and fired a second time. The strange mewling noise leaking from his cousin ceased.

Zoe lowered her head to her hands and began rocking back and forth. Lee blinked at his missing finger. Not knowing what else to do, he clamped it tight in his armpit to staunch the bleeding.

He tried not to look at his cousin but the pull was too great. A wisp of steam was rising from the flayed flesh of the body. Lee looked away.

She kept rocking and rocking. He asked if she was all right, but she didn't answer.

Time lost all meaning, like a black spell cast over the forgotten cemetery. It was broken by the clomp of boots approaching from the south. Elvis materialized in the weak light of the abandoned flashlights. A forelock of dyed black hair had fallen loose, bobbing over his brow as he surveyed the destruction at his feet.

"Shit and fried eggs," he said.

Lee felt his blasted hand awake with fresh pain. "We need a doctor," he said to the man with the bobbing lock.

Elvis went down on one knee to study the mortal remains sprawled against the stone. He turned away and poked the toe of his boot against the lumpen sacks of treasure on the ground. A handful of coins had spilled onto the sand. Elvis selected one and held it up to the light. "It is pretty, ain't it? The way it catches the light like that."

Zoe gaped at the man, stammering until her voice returned. "Did you hear him? He needs help."

The King turned, looked at her and then looked at him. "He'll live."

The bullfrogs in the creek had resumed their chorus and the moon shone down on all of them. Uncle Elvis tossed the coin back into the satchel, cinched the cord tight, and dragged both sacks along the dirt to the edge of the open pit. And then he dropped them both into the grave of poor Albert Walker.

Lee sank, his head lowering but Zoe's eyes widened in confusion. "What the hell are you doing?" she demanded.

"You think you're the first to go after this thing?" He scanned the ground where a few of the coins had fallen loose. He kicked them into the grave. "Every generation, some dumb-ass goes digging for it."

"You can't," uttered Zoe, slack-jawed as the last of the treasure vanished into the earth. "After all this?"

The King ignored her, tying a bow on the whole damn thing. "And every time it ends badly."

Her hands clamped over her head as if pressure was building from within her skull. "Christ, what the hell was it all for?"

"The only place for this damned thing is back in the ground," Elvis said.

The antique Smith & Wesson lay with its barrel in the sand, the mahogany grip-piece still clutched in the dead hand. Elvis pried the revolver loose and broke it at the hinge, shaking the spent casing into his palm. "Your granddad found it," he said. "Did you know that? He and old uncle Frank, they were determined. And the minute they hauled it up, they turned on each other."

The spent casings rattled in his palm like dice. He pitched them into the grave.

"Your granddad got shot in the foot but he managed to stove Frank's brain with a rock. Then he pitched the body into a well. But the wound in his foot was too much. Shock kicked in, triggering the stroke."

Lee shuddered, his chin lowering to hide his tears. Zoe had some fight yet in her, trying to process the nightmare. She crawled toward the graveside. "This was all for nothing?"

The older man blocked her way. He held the pistol by the barrel. "One more inch and I'll dash your brains in."

She scuttled back. Elvis tossed the gun into the grave. It landed with a crack against the coffin. "I'll get you two to the hospital once we're done here. Officer Phil is gonna have some questions.

No way around that." When Lee didn't react, he kicked the boy's foot and squared him with a hard look. "You're gonna tell our friend Phil that you blew your finger off playing with a gun. You got that?"

Lee wiped a hand over his sticky face. He turned to look at the body sprawled in the clover. "What about Truman? I shot him."

"No, you didn't," Elvis stated. "Your cousin Truman ran away from home and vanished. Just like Uncle Frank."

Bending low, he gripped a limp arm and dragged Truman to the edge of the grave. His boot heel slotted against the dead boy's ribs and he rolled the body over the side.

Zoe closed her eyes and started rocking again. Lee watched the older man take up a spade and plunge it into the mound of dirt, backfilling the hole.

"On your feet, boys and girls," Elvis said. "There's another spade over there. You two dug up this mess, you can help bury it, too."

Lee put one hand on his knee and forced himself upright. Zoe didn't move.

"Hey," he said.

She lifted her head and wiped her eyes. Saw the hand held out to her. Taking it, she let him haul her to her feet and they bent to their task.

Suddenly, last summer

THE RIVER WAS green and dark. Sometimes after a heavy rainfall, the water would turn a muddy brown. It was never blue, never that turquoise ripple of a tropical paradise but it was the closest he had experienced and, as is the way with these things, it was only appreciated when it was gone. Last summer, during an August heatwave. Two weeks before she left for university.

Under a rusting span bridge over Snake River, they had peeled out of their clothes and cannonballed into the green water. A shady spot he called the Gulch, where the trees canopied over an old dock jutting out into the creek. A record spike in the heat had fizzled everything to a slow churn but the overhanging trees shaded them as they splashed about in the slow-moving water.

Flopping back onto the dock, they took turns critiquing each other's plunge into the water. Lee stuck to the cannonball, intent on making the biggest splash possible. She graded it a seven for effort. Then he hauled himself onto the boards to judge her attempt.

Zoe vaulted into the humid air and arced gracefully into a clean dive, back straight and toes pointed. He was predisposed to granting her a perfect score on a belly-flop but his judgment was true.

"A ten!" he cheered, clapping when her head broke the surface.

"Felt more like an eight to me," she said, gliding back to the dock. "Was my back straight?"

"From my perspective, it was perfect."

Zoe draped her arms over the lip of the dock and bopped her fist against his thigh. "Perv."

He couldn't wipe the grin from his face. "Go again?"

The muscles in her arms popped as she pushed out of the water and onto the dock. Raking her hair back over her scalp, she said: "How about a cocktail first?"

The beer dangled underwater, suspended from the dock on a length of twine. They cracked two open and lay back to dry on the warm, splintery boards of the dock. Sunlight dappled through the leafy boughs dipping above them.

They had done it twice already, both experiences leaving them flushed and confused. The first time on the flat roof of the concession stand at the abandoned drive-in theatre, almost two weeks ago. They had gone to watch the Perseid meteor shower. At the first blazing scratch across the night sky, he had asked what she wished for but she had said that wishes had to be secret. He disagreed. Secrets were irrelevant to a falling star. It either granted the wish or didn't. A smirk stole over her face. She said that she wished she could feel happiness like this all the time, and not just these tiny fragmented moments. Then she asked what he had wished for but it was written all over his face. Lee would never be a poker player.

Awkward, giddy and searingly self-conscious. But something more than that, something neither knew how to articulate. Afterward, they had dressed quickly in a confused vapor of bliss and shame.

The confusion remained over the next few days until they met at a house party out on the far side of town. While the party raged on in the backyard, the two of them slipped out to the front porch where it was quiet. The clumsiness fell away as they prattled on in a hushed tone and then kissed like it was an emergency. Hearing someone approach, they broke off and rejoined the party, spending the rest of the night trying to act normal, smirking occasionally over a shared secret.

He asked if she wanted to go swimming. He knew a spot on Snake River that he called the Gulch. No one ever went there, he'd said, adding that it was the best place to cool off on a hot day. Splashing and teasing and flirting, they had fallen into it like a dream or a fever. There was less fumbling but the confusion afterward lingered. What were they doing? Were they insane? Sick? Neither knew, but neither pressed the issue.

So this third time, lying side by side and naked in the dappled sunlight. They talked about nothing, teasing and flirting and letting the tension coil to an almost unbearable level. But the difference that last time, when they had rolled onto their sides and their lips met, was that there had been no fumbling or frantic questioning about what they were doing. Both were desperate to connect in the rawest way they knew how. Both stopped asking themselves why this had happened, or how. Those questions were too big. It had simply happened and it wouldn't last.

They lay their heads back down on the dock and spoke about their dreams, the big ones, all blue-sky thinking. Careers and ambitions, big cities and faraway locations. Rumbling under all their dreams was the notion of escape and possible reinvention. Carving away the old identity in a new place and crafting a new one. One that fit better than the self they were born into.

The river churning lazily below, Zoe turned to him. "You were right."

"About what?"

"This. The gulch." She turned her face back to the sky and closed her eyes. "It's perfect. Does anyone else know about it?"

He traced a fingertip along her bicep. Her skin was clammy from the river, rough with gooseflesh. "Aside from the guy who built this dock, I doubt it."

"Then how do you know it's called the gulch?"

"Just a name I made up."

She smiled. The phantom dimple on her left cheek made a brief appearance. "We could spend the rest of the summer here. Away from everything."

"Works for me. We could fish out of the river. Build a fire on the bank. All we need."

The rest of the summer. There was barely a week left of it and he didn't want to think about what followed. She was off to university while he was stranded here for his last year of high school.

He leaned up on one elbow and counted the freckles on her shoulder. "You worried?"

"About what?" She cupped a hand over her eyes to block the sunlight. "Us?"

"No, university. New school, new town. All that."

She closed her eyes again, a faint smile tugging the corners of her mouth. "I can't wait."

He was about to suggest that he could come visit her but then decided against it. It would sound needy and it would spoil the moment, so he lay back down on the hard boards and kept quiet. Her fingers curled into his.

She sat up and looked down at the water. "One more splash? Then we should go."

He agreed and they jumped into the river again, the water bracing on their skin.

34

Frontier days - Sipping margaritas - There is no romance at the bus station - Departure time - No face in the window - Passing the mantle - An unwanted apprenticeship - The gentlemanly sport of crow shooting

THE DAYS GREW cloyed with lazy heat and by mid-July, it had all blown over. The sun rose and fell on the little town like nothing had ever happened. The police investigation died down, Officer Phil Carson satisfied with the general assumption that Truman Traven had simply run off like he'd always claimed he would. Most who knew him accepted it. The only dissenter was Truman's mother but the more she insisted that something had happened to her son, the more she was dismissed as hysterical.

Aunt Carol had always been a bit nutty, they whispered. Hadn't she?

Mid-summer brought with it the town's annual Frontier Days Festival where townsfolk donned cowboy hats or petticoats to reenact some Wild West version of history that never was. A faux rodeo of fiddle music, square dancing and mock shootouts with pop guns. A good time was had, but not by all.

Lee stayed home, avoiding the fairgrounds. As did Zoe and Jeremy.

Jeremy came to believe the story of Truman's escape with each passing day. He imagined his cousin sipping margaritas on a beach or living large somewhere glitzy like New York City. When he saw Zoe in town, he crossed to the other side of the street to avoid her. At hockey practice, he didn't even look at Lee and after a week, he stopped going to practice altogether. It was clear that neither of their circumstances had changed.

So Truman had fled with the loot after all and, maybe, Jeremy thought, one day he'd get a call from his wayward cousin, inviting him to come visit. That made it easier to believe, that little green shoot of hope. The alternate theory was simply too awful to consider.

<hr />

The bus for Kingston departed at 4:30 PM on Saturday. Lee went to see her off. They sat on a dusty bench and watched the bus pull in and dock. A few haggard riders stumbled out and then the driver announced the departure in five minutes.

"This is me."

Zoe pushed herself up and hoisted the heavy backpack onto her shoulder.

They had barely spoken over the last few weeks. Like Jeremy, they had avoided one another. Three nights ago, Lee was surprised to see her number pop up on his phone. Zoe called to say that she was going back to university after all. In fact, she was leaving town as soon as possible.

The Traven farm had sold. While the chattels on the property, such as the equipment and the contents of the house, were still contested among the inheritors, the land itself had sold to developer Big Bill Daggett. Daggett's outfit had already begun bulldozing the property and Daggett strutted through town like a conquering hero, tipping his white Stetson to everyone on the street.

The money from the purchase, once divided amongst them, was enough to mitigate the cost of caring for her dad and allow Zoe one more year of university. It wouldn't be easy, and Zoe would have to work part-time to cover her rent, but it was doable. And she was leaving right away. Kingston was a university town, bustling with students during the school year but quiet in the summer months. Moving back in mid-summer meant she could secure a couple of part-time jobs and have her pick of the cheapest flats close to campus.

She had called to say goodbye. When he learned she was taking the bus, he asked to see her off.

Sitting on the bench outside the dingy bus station, they had said little. She asked about his injured hand. He said it was healing but it felt strange. He could still feel the missing finger. She told him it was phantom pain and that it was common. They talked about her plans once she got back to Kingston and how cheaply she'd have to live during the school year. Neither of them mentioned anything about lost treasures or the graves of dead children or the guns of fabled outlaws. The closest they came to broaching the subject was speculating about Jeremy.

He asked if she had spoken to him. She hadn't, admitting that she would duck out of sight when she saw him on the street. Lee told her that their cousin had stopped going to practice with the Sharks. Had he quit the team? He didn't know.

They crossed the platform and Zoe stowed her backpack into the luggage compartment. A few people had boarded the Greyhound and the driver stood at the door, casting an eye for any stragglers.

Lee wanted to stall the moment but the driver was already closing the hatch to the luggage compartment. He looked at Zoe. When she smiled, he had hoped to catch one last glimpse of the rare phantom dimple but it failed to appear on her cheek. He wondered if it was gone forever, given the events of that night, and the thought of it vanishing forever seemed like the saddest thing he ever heard of.

He looked at the ground and then up at her again. "I guess I won't see you till Christmas break, huh?"

"Maybe," she said with a shrug.

The bus driver cleared his throat, trying to be polite.

Zoe glanced at the bus and then back to Lee. "I won't be back at Christmas."

"You're not ever coming back. Are you?"

"No."

The driver broke the silence. "We're pulling out, miss," he said.

Zoe ran a hand through her hair. "I don't know what to say."

"Me neither," he replied.

An embrace. Awkward and quick and over.

"Okay," she said and scampered onto the bus. The door swung closed with a pneumatic hiss and the bus rolled away from the concrete curb.

Lee gave a little wave but he couldn't see her through the tinted windows. He couldn't see any passengers at all, just the dim outline of the seats, as if the bus was empty.

———— ◆◆◇◆◆ ————

Main Street was dusty and hot with dregs of straw still clotted along the curbside from the bales brought in for the Frontier Days Festival. Chaff drifted around his ankles as Lee crossed the street to the battered Ford pickup truck waiting for him. The door squealed on its hinge as he climbed in and Uncle Elvis turned the ignition.

They watched the Greyhound bus roll out of Garrison Street onto the main drag and rumble out of town.

Elvis nodded at the coach, billowing black exhaust as it picked up speed. "She on her way?"

"Yeah."

The older man pulled the stick into gear and studied his passenger.

"You all right?"

"Yeah."

They rolled leisurely along Main Street, past the same storefronts that never seemed to change. Looking out the passenger window, Lee noted the 'For Lease' sign in the window of the old bookshop. Even that never seemed to change, as if the shop was cursed to never find a new proprietor.

"You know," Elvis remarked, "this town ain't so bad. You'll find your way."

Lee jostled in his seat when the truck hit a patch of uneven pavement. He said nothing.

Elvis went on. "Life's a bit easier if you have a sense of purpose. Like keeping vigil or standing watch over something." He spun the wheel, turning onto Albany Street. "Think of it as a calling."

"A calling?"

"A calling."

Lee watched the street pass by. The role of sentinel. He was being groomed to be the next one, apprentice to a vigil he had not asked for but could not refuse now. In the grander sweep of things, he was getting off easy, he supposed.

The buildings of town faded behind them as the truck rolled onto Highway 9. Crows dotted the power lines that ran parallel to the road. Elvis pointed the blackbirds out to his passenger.

"Jesus, look at them damn things. You ever gone crow shooting, Lee?"

The crows on the line seem to turn and watch the truck pass below them. Lee settled back into the seat. "Isn't that a crime, shooting crows?"

"It's only a crime if you're caught," said the King. He bopped the boy's shoulder with a light rabbit-tap. "I'll teach you."

They drove on.

The boring Afterword

(feel free to skip this part)

THANKS for reading *Just Like Jesse James*. This book has been a bit of a life-saver for me. Back in May I released the eighth book in the Spookshow series and was trying to figure out where the story would go from there. I toyed with the idea of ending the series, wrapping it all up in two more books, but then I choked. A weird pressure came over me, trying to envision a satisfying finale to the book series I'd spent two years working on and I folded. Every idea I came up with was terrible and unworthy of the series thus far. What I needed was a break.

Before I started writing novels, I used to write movies. Of the stack of unproduced screenplays I had penned, there was a handful of scripts that I still liked and wanted to turn into novels. Now was the time to take a stab at it. Digging it out those old scripts, I read through one but became quickly dispirited. The story just wasn't up to snuff, so I put it aside and opened the weird one about cousins on a treasure hunt. It still worked. In fact, it was better than I had remembered. I happily dove in.

The initial idea came from a kid's book about Canadian legends and ghost stories; two short paragraphs about a fortune in gold buried on a farm in small town Ontario by Jesse James. I'm a sucker for folktales like that but it seemed so improbable. There is no evidence that the famous outlaw ever crossed the border into Canada. Why would he? A die-hard Confederate to the very end, James would have had no interest in scouting north to the wilds of what was then the British Empire. The same legend about Jame's lost treasure exists through countless parts of the U.S. so it would have made more sense to set the story down south, but it was the very outlandishness of the idea that appealed to me, so I kept the tale set in rural Ontario.

If you're interested in the history of Jesse James, I highly recommend *Jesse James: Last Rebel of the Civil War* by T. J. Stiles. Impeccably researched and masterfully told, it is a delight to read. Some biographers have a magic touch combining historical facts and insights with a thrilling narrative pace. Stiles is among the best.

To be honest, I don't know if this strange treasure hunt novel will appeal to anyone other than myself. It's ultimately about family and it doesn't have a lot of nice things to say on that topic. Plus the subplot between Lee and Zoe might, understandably, repulse some readers. I doubt this book will do well in sales or readership but that's okay. It's a passion project that I had a lot of fun writing and it's helped to clear my head so I can get back to the Spookshow series with a fresh eye.

Thanks again for reading.

Toronto
October, 2017

Tim McGregor is an author and screenwriter. He lives in Toronto with his wife and children. Some days he believes in ghosts, other days not so much.

He can be reached at timmcgregorauthor.com

www.ingramcontent.com/pod-product-compliance
Lightning Source LLC
Chambersburg PA
CBHW020236180626
46810CB00006B/2229